NIGHT DROP

A PINX VIDEO MYSTERY

MARSHALL THORNTON

KENMORE BOOKS

Published by Kenmore Books
Edited by Joan Martinelli
Cover design by Marshall Thornton
Images by 123rf stock
ISBN-13: 978-1973782315
ISBN-10: 1973782316

First Edition

I would like to thank Joan Martinelli, Randy and Valerie Trumbull, Kevin E. Davis, Nathan Bay, Mark Jewkes and Louis Dumser, Robin Sinclair, and Helene Augustyniak.

———————

LOOKING BACK, IT SEEMS ODD THAT I OPENED THE STORE the second day of the riots, but that morning we weren't especially afraid. The horrible things that were happening were all happening far from Silver Lake. No one I talked to the night before was afraid for themselves. Even the *LA Times* seemed to take an optimistic tone. The newspaper box chained to a lamppost in front of my store boasted the headline VIOLENCE ERUPTS. Violence that erupted could just as easily collapse. But a riot, the word they'd so carefully avoided—though the TV stations had not—a riot raged and roared until it burned itself out.

Pinx Video was on Hyperion in a little stretch of storefronts with a dry cleaner on one side, a takeout place called Taco Maria on the other, and a gas station across the street. Large, plate glass windows ran across the front of the building, but there were no windows on either side or in the back. And, no, our storefront was not pink. The landlord had refused to let us change its dusty blue, but we did hang a pink neon sign in the center window. It said PINX VIDEO in all capital letters and beneath in turquoise 3-Day Rental.

My late—my late what? I never knew how to talk about Jeffer Cole. I suppose I could say he was my late boyfriend, though that lessened the relationship. My late lover sounded like a tragic romance novel—Read *My Late Lover* and bawl your eyes out! My late partner sounded like we were in business together, and though we were that too, it made me feel like I was trying to hide something. My late husband was the one that felt right, but I had no legal claim to it. Usually, I went to great lengths to avoid the phrase entirely.

Jeffer and I had opened Pinx Video together in eighty-nine. The name was his idea. Pink because we wanted to stock a lot of gay movies. But ending in an X because we wanted to stock a lot of gay *porno* movies. Actually, Jeffer originally wanted to call it Pinxxx, but I put my foot down. All those Xs seemed vulgar. As though we planned to *only* rent porno movies.

It was ten o'clock when I walked in. We didn't open until eleven, but Mikey Kellerman was already behind the front counter dutifully counting out the cash drawers. In his mid-thirties, he had pale brown hair that he was losing quickly. He wore a blue T-shirt with thin green horizontal stripes, a pair of jeans with a slit over the right knee, and Doc Martens. Over his heart, he wore a small, black Silence = Death pin.

A television sat on a raised shelf on the counter behind him. Normally, we only used it to check damaged videos or to play titles that weren't moving—hoping to tempt the browsers. It wasn't even hooked up to cable. Mikey had pulled up the antenna and it played a snowy version of the local news. They were showing scenes of people being dragged from vehicles the night before.

Following my eyes to the television, Mikey said, "I hope that's okay. I thought we should know what's happening."

"It's fine," I said. "Just maybe not when the customers start coming in. The sooner everyone forgets about what happened, the better."

"What happened? It sounds like it's still happening."

"I'm sure they've got everything under control," I said, naively.

"That's not what they're saying."

"It's not stopping?"

2

"It's spreading. Five people have died."

"Turn the sound up."

The news anchor, who looked tired and stressed and had likely been talking for hours, said, "We're getting word that the mayor has expanded the curfew area beyond the South Central area to all parts of the city. There have been reports of looting in Culver City, Van Nuys and along Santa Monica Boulevard in Hollywood."

For the first time, I wondered whether or not we should open the store for business. I wondered whether or not we were safe.

"Do you think we should open today or not?"

Mikey didn't hesitate. "No. We shouldn't."

"I think you're right. You can take off if you want. I'll call people and let them know not to come in."

"Oh no. I should stay and help protect the store."

The store wasn't much more than a big room with three rows of shelved video boxes. There was a small office, a bathroom for employees and a storage room behind the counter where we kept the actual videos in plastic boxes: black for general releases, brown for porn.

"I don't think we need to do that," I said. "I doubt anything will happen and even it does, everything's insured." And I had no idea how I'd go about protecting the store even if I wanted to. "There's really nothing in here except a few hundred plastic boxes and a lot of used videos."

"It's your business, though. You and Jeffer created it. Doesn't it mean anything to you?"

I didn't have time to think about what Pinx Video did or did not mean to me since apparently we were in the middle of a riot, so I said, "I think your safety and the safety of everyone who works here is more—"

"Do you have a gun? That's what they're doing in Koreatown. Standing on their roofs with guns."

"Of course, I don't have a gun. And even if I did, I wouldn't get up on the roof—"

"Do you know anyone who does? Can you borrow a gun?"

3

he said, as though we were discussing a cup of sugar needed for his favorite cookie recipe.

"No. I'm not going to borrow a gun." He got a look on his face. One I'd seen before. "And neither are you."

It wouldn't be the first time he did what he thought was in the store's best interest whether I liked it or not.

"Then what are you going to do?"

"Go home. We're just going to lock up and go home. Who's supposed to come in today?"

"Mindy's on at noon. Carl and Denny at four."

"All right. I'll call them. Put the cash drawers back in the office."

"You should probably take them home, don't you think?"

It hardly mattered. Each drawer held two-hundred and fifty dollars in change. Like everything else, the money was insured. It barely seemed worth the trouble to bring them home. I shook my head and said, "Just put them in the office."

After I'd called everyone, I tried again to get Mikey to leave. "You should go home and stay there. Is Randy at the hospital?" Mikey's boyfriend was a nurse at County.

"He's been there since yesterday. Doesn't know when he'll be home."

"That many people have been injured?"

"A lot of injuries, yes. But a lot of heart attacks, too. People are having heart attacks just because they're scared."

It was terrible to think about, things were so bad people were dying from fright.

"If it gets any worse you should go down to the hospital with Randy. I'm sure it'll be safe there, and they could probably use the help."

He frowned at me. "We should do something about the computers."

On the front counter were two computers set up with custom software to check out customers. There was a third in my little office. There was also a dot matrix printer for printing out receipts. The whole system was connected by a maze of cords, which made disconnecting them (and eventually re-connecting them) a nightmare.

"We'll just pull the shades." There were transparent, tinted plastic shades meant to block the afternoon heat. They cast a gray film on the place and you could still see in. Just not well.

Mikey gave me his look. "I'm putting the computers on the floor, at least."

"Fine. And then we're leaving."

Sometimes I felt like a ghost.

I met Jeffer when I was twenty-two. I'd moved out to Los Angeles from Michigan with the idea of doing something in show business. I loved movies, but I didn't like people looking at me so I never wanted to be an actor. I also wasn't exactly creative, and that put a lot of showbiz jobs out of reach. Well, most.

I had a bachelor's degree in business, though to be honest, after four years of study I wasn't entirely sure what business was about other than common sense. Most of my classes stated such obvious things I had trouble staying awake. The main benefit of my education turned out to be the offer of a couch to sleep on in Studio City.

In the back of *Drama-Logue*, I found an ad for a production assistant on a low-budget movie. I answered it. The pay barely covered the cost of gasoline, but I did meet Jeffer Cole. He was the production designer, almost ten years my senior and about the most attractive man I'd ever seen in person. I went from my friend's couch to Jeffer's bed and never left. Well, not until the end. I did leave at the end.

For a couple of years I waited tables, while Jeffer became increasingly successful. At first, I made more than he did on a regular basis, but by the end of our first year he was working all the time and out earning me by leaps and bounds. In eighty-eight, we bought a house, something that was almost inconceivable to me at twenty-four, and then, the next year, we started

Pinx Video. At twenty-five, I was a businessman, a homeowner and a devoted partner. Life was perfect. For about a year.

At times I felt like a ghost. I think I hadn't had enough time to become myself before I met Jeffer, and then I was part of Noah and Jeffer, Jeffer and Noah. We went to a party once and I overheard someone saying about me, "It's like he has no personality when Jeffer leaves the room." It was a cruel thing to say, mostly because it felt true.

That's what I was thinking about as I drove home in a riot. *Strange,* I thought. *Very strange.* But then I remembered it was almost the anniversary of Jeffer's getting sick; the great unraveling of secrets and lies; the beginning of my floating away from him, ghostlike and empty.

My apartment was less than a mile from Pinx Video. Around the time Jeffers died, I'd moved to a small, one-bedroom apartment on a hill in Silver Lake. Not one of the better hills, a hill well below Sunset. The good part of Silver Lake was north of Sunset surrounding the actual lake, of course. Fanning out from there were some decent blocks, but then, when you crossed Sunset, you came to a hilly area where altitude and income fell into step. The wealthier people lived at the top of the hills, while the poor and desperate lived at the bottom.

Not that my apartment was the kind of place where rich people lived. The dishwater gray building was a small six-unit L wrapped around a shabby, old-growth courtyard. There were thick, shaggy palms, birds of paradise and a dribbling fountain, leaving only enough room for a single metal table and chairs. A cement stairway—painted rusty red—came up from the street and garages to the courtyard, then a wooden stairway led to the second floor. A red-tiled walkway with white railings ran across the entire second floor.

My place was on the second floor at the front giving me a southwest view of the basin. As I was unlocking my door that morning, I glanced out and saw plumes of smoke rising above the city in at least a dozen spots. I suppose most of them had been there when I'd left two hours before, but I hadn't thought much about them, assuming they were left over from the night before. Now they seemed ominous; a hint of the future rather than a glimpse of the past.

I wasn't sure if the apartment measured six hundred square feet, if it did it was just that. The living room was small, too small for a full sofa so I had a second-hand love seat that I'd wrapped in a crazy black and purple print I'd gotten at the new IKEA in Burbank. Beside that there wasn't much other than a black leather chair with a bent-wood frame—also from IKEA, it was called POONG or something unpronounceable along those lines—a veneered armoire from the thirties which held my 13-inch TV/VCR combo, my video collection (or at least part of it), a compact stereo and a stack of CDs I'd gotten from a record club. On the wall over the POONG chair hung a Hockney poster that Jeffer had bought me at the LACMA retrospective in eighty-eight.

There was a faux Danish modern dinette set that I'd put in front of the window next to the dining area off the kitchen. That area was too small for the table, so I'd turned it into an office area by putting my sixties-style metal desk under the corner windows.

The minuscule, U-shaped kitchen had appliances that were brand new when I was in high school and very little counter space, most of which was taken up by my most important appliance, the microwave.

The bedroom had a wall of closets, and a wall of built-in cabinets and drawers, leaving exactly enough room for a queen-sized bed. I had set my bed in front of a do-it-yourself bookcase made of concrete blocks and planks of wood, using it as a kind of headboard. This eliminated the need for nightstands, which there wasn't room for anyway. I'd painted the entire apartment dove gray and put in bright white miniblinds. I ignored the sculptured brown carpet as best I could.

I put on a Dionne Warwick CD and kicked off my shoes. I went into the bathroom to wash my face. I don't think it was dirty, but just the idea of a riot made everything seem sooty and thick. I tried not to look at myself. If I had I would not have seen the ghost I felt like but instead a reasonably attractive young man of around twenty-eight. I had brown eyes and unremarkable but symmetrical features. The most noticeable thing about me was my hair. It was massively thick and stubborn. It did whatever it chose and I had little say in the matter. I'd tried every product out there and nothing tamed the beast on my head. At that particular moment it needed cutting, but I could hardly put out a bulletin to stop the riot so I could find a barber.

I tried even harder not to look at the rest of me. If you were being unkind you'd call me delicate, frail, skinny—I couldn't for the life of me keep weight on—elf-like even. And if you were being kind, well, there were few kind words for a man of my stature.

Dionne was nearly finished loving Paris when the phone rang. I pressed pause on the CD player and picked up the cordless. It was Louis from downstairs.

"Marc is on his way home from the studio. They're shutting down. Did you close the video store?"

"I did."

"Good idea. I'm making lunch. Come down."

I'd barely said yes when he hung up. Louis was partial to short telephone chats and long after-dinner conversations. I didn't need to change my clothes; I dressed casually at Pinx— though not as casually as my employees. Still, I changed into a pair of khaki shorts, flip-flops, a mock turtleneck and an oversized jean jacket. I ran a comb through my hair but quickly gave up trying to subdue it. Then went down to the courtyard about ten minutes later.

Louis had a glass of chardonnay already poured for me. The sky was thick with clouds—the marine layer—but that didn't matter. There was an umbrella stuck into the center of the metal table in the extremely remote chance it rained.

Sitting on the ground next to the table was a high-end boom box tuned to KCRW. They were discussing whether the Federal government might now file charges against the LAPD officers accused of beating King. The guest was fairly certain they would.

"We live in strange times," Louis said coming out of his apartment. He and Marc lived directly below in an apartment that was identically small. While I had a view, they'd claimed this end of the courtyard for themselves.

Wearing navy shorts, penny loafers, a light blue dress shirt and an apron that said "Finger Lickin' Good," Louis was tall, nearly forty and spreading in the middle. His eyes protruded a bit and his smile was wide, giving him the look of a jovial frog. I wasn't the first to notice it; there was a collection of miniature frogs on his kitchen windowsill. In one hand he held a plate full of uncooked ribs.

"We live in strange times, so you thought you'd barbecue?" I asked.

"It was that or pack up the car and flee."

He set the ribs on the table and bent over a small hibachi. In a short while, he had the coals lit and sat down with me at the table.

"So. Can you believe the verdict?" he asked.

"It was shocking."

"I don't see how they could come to that decision. Between the videotape and Gates himself saying it was…what was the word he used, an aberration?"

I sipped the wine. It was cold, sweet and tart at the same time, and warming as it went down. The glass had sprouted beads of water. I rubbed at them while I listened to the sirens in the distance.

"I don't remember much about the beating. I wasn't paying attention," I admitted.

"Well, it wasn't an aberration. I've seen the LAPD beat people like that before."

"You have?"

"Absolutely. I mean, there was no video camera handy. And the person was white. But you have to know LAPD makes a habit of this."

"So, it's systemic?"

"Again, the video. Look at all those other cops standing around watching, doing nothing. That's systemic."

"What about people saying King was on PCP?"

"And it gives you superhuman strength?"

I shrugged. That's what they said, but I had no idea.

"If that man had superhuman strength they left it out of the video," Louis said.

Just then, Marc came up the stairs. He was smaller and wider than Louis, and about ten years younger. He wore gray wool slacks, a white shirt and a red tie. In one hand, he carried the jacket that went with the slacks, in the other a scuffed brief-case. His face was round and his lips were what my mother's generation would have called bee-stung.

Not bothering to go inside, he flopped down in one chair and tossed his things in another, before he pulled out a pack of extra-long menthol cigarettes.

"Oh. My. God. I just drove through hell." He lit his cigarette and inhaled. "I took Washington to Vermont, my normal route. Huge mistake. I had no idea that South Central was like a block away from there. A block! They started talking about it on the radio. Did you know that it goes all the way up to the 10? I certainly didn't. And there I was, a block from the 10. And then, almost as soon as I realize that, I glance over and there are these guys trying to break into a liquor store on the other side of the street. I mean, the place had all these security bars and they're just ripping them down like they're curtains—Louis, why haven't you gotten me a glass of wine?"

"Well dear, it seemed rude to walk away while you were talking."

"Go get me wine. I'll talk louder." He inhaled deeply from his cigarette. "So, every few blocks there's someone trying to break into a business and then…OH MY GOD!" he yelled so Louis could hear him inside. "I get to Washington and Vermont and there are two, not one but TWO GAS STATIONS ON FIRE!"

Louis came out of the apartment with a fresh glass of wine

for himself and one for Marc. "You didn't stop for any red lights, did you?"

"Are you crazy? Not after the things we saw on TV last night." He took the glass of wine. "Oh thank God." After a long sip, he continued. "I don't know what happened. This morning —I mean, I drove the same route at eight-thirty—nothing was happening, nothing was being broken into, and nothing was on fire."

"I guess rioters like to sleep in," Louis suggested. "They were up late last night, after all."

"Did you really run red lights?" I asked.

"Only the one at Washington and Vermont."

"So, there were no fire engines at that intersection? No police?"

"No, the gas stations were just burning."

"Well," said Louis. "We're glad you made it home safe."

"Yes, my being dragged from the car and beaten would have ruined your appetite."

"Well, it would have," Louis said. "Though not as much as worrying about how I'd get the Infiniti back." He looked at me and said, "It's on a lease."

I enjoyed Marc and Louis and their banter. I felt safe with them for some reason. I wondered what Jeffer would have thought of them. I doubt he'd have liked them. I remember the first time I brought Jeffer up, Marc said, "Good God, what kind of a name is Jeffer?"

"He was Jeff as a child. And then Jeffrey. But he liked Jeffer best."

"Pretentious," Marc said.

"Now, now," Louis interrupted. "Don't speak ill of the dead. Not when there are living people you can speak ill of." And then he did just that, taking a few swipes at the president, who I found too bland to be worth insulting, or Pat Robertson or the mayor. It was fine with me, of course, since I preferred to talk about anything but Jeffer.

"Did you close the video store?" Marc asked.

"Of course, he closed the video store," Louis replied for me.

"He's here isn't he? He wouldn't just leave his employees to fend for themselves."

"Do you think it will be all right?" Marc asked, pointedly ignoring his lover.

"Well, they're not sure it's going to get this far," I said. "I've heard most of it is still happening in South Central and Koreatown."

"Yes, I imagine Koreatown's getting slammed," Louis said. "It's one thing to murder a child. It's another to get off scot-free."

"It was involuntary manslaughter," Marc corrected.

"You say potato I say murder."

White flakes of ash began falling through the air. One or two at first, then more. The wind picked them up somewhere nearby. A somewhere nearby that was on fire.

"And Korea*town* didn't kill the girl, that cashier did. It's not the neighborhood's fault. It's really the judge's fault, she's the one who reduced the sentence. They should go burn her house down and be done with it."

"And the jury out in Simi Valley. They should get their houses burned down. Come to think of it, they can burn the whole Simi Valley."

"I blame public transportation," I said quietly.

"What?" Louis asked, and they both looked at me.

"Public transportation is terrible in L.A. The rioters can't get to Simi Valley."

Louis erupted into laughter. He put the ribs onto the hibachi, and when he stood up noticed the white flakes of ash floating in the air.

"Huh. Who says it never snows in Los Angeles."

2

AFTER LUNCH, WE HAD AT LEAST TWO BOTTLES OF WINE and chewed over everything that had led up to the riots. It seemed, from what they were saying on the radio, the LAPD had not been prepared. Louis thought this deplorable, while Marc made the interesting point that Chief Gates probably thought the officers would be convicted of *something*. If they'd been convicted of *something, anything*—even disturbing the peace—the city might not be burning itself down.

Eventually, I crawled upstairs and took a two-hour nap. It would have been longer if the phone hadn't rung. And rung. And rung. My mother was calling from Grand Rapids. The sun had gone down so I lurched around the living room and turned on a light.

"Are you all right?" she asked, breathless. "You didn't return my calls. I was worried." She'd called three times the first night of the riot. I didn't mean to be cruel, I just had a habit of avoiding my mother whenever things got challenging. And a riot qualified as challenging.

"I'm sorry about that. But I'm fine." Aside from an early evening hangover.

"The things they're showing on television. I don't know if I'm going to be able to sleep."

I stepped over to the armoire and turned on the TV. My best reception was channel 2. It wasn't great, but I could make out what was happening. And what was happening just then was a Circuit City being looted. I was fairly certain it was one on Sunset just blocks away.

"I'm safe. And I'm going to stay that way."

"Did you see them pull that man out of his truck yesterday? Horrible, just horrible."

"It was horrible."

"I keep expecting to see your little video store on the TV."

"I think the store will be fine."

"How can people behave like that?"

She had not asked the same question of the beating. Like many people, she'd assumed if the police beat you up you'd done something to deserve it. Of course, guilty people didn't deserve to be beaten, that wasn't how our system was supposed to work. Even if you *were* found guilty, a judge wouldn't sentence you to a beating. It was barbaric.

"They're angry," I said. "They don't believe they got justice."

"But, do you really think they let those men off just because they're white?"

Honestly, I didn't know. I hadn't paid attention to the trial. But it was hard not to agree with Marc that they should have been convicted of something.

"Can you look at the video of the beating and tell me they didn't do something wrong?" I asked.

"It does *look* bad. But then, two wrongs don't make a right." I didn't know whether she meant the beating and the verdict, or the verdict and the rioting. It didn't matter, since she changed the subject. "You're staying inside, aren't you?"

"Yes, I'm staying inside." Except for getting drunk in the courtyard, of course.

"I suppose we should be glad Jeffer didn't live to see this."

I had no idea what to make of that. I'm sure he would have survived the riot just fine. But then I knew she adored Jeffer. She brought him up often. When he passed, she'd asked, "Oh dear, how will you ever find anyone as nice as Jeffer?"

As it happened, he wasn't nicer than other people, he'd just made an effort to charm my mother. Not knowing what else to say, I said, "Yeah."

"Oh, I forgot to tell you. I volunteered for the Cancer Society of America. In honor of Jeffers."

"That's nice."

"Jeannie Shaver is doing it with me."

"Uh-huh."

On my TV, some guy was dragging a huge big-screen TV out of Circuit City. The thing was, he was dragging it screen down. It would be completely ruined after only a few feet. If he managed to get it home, it wouldn't be worth watching. I wondered what the point was.

"Of course, I don't know what they'll ask us to do. I mean, I hope it's nothing too difficult. I wouldn't mind reading to people in the hospital. You know, to take their minds off—"

"Mom, it's late."

"It's not late there. It's late here. Oh, wait, did I screw up again. I can never get this right. Is it three hours earlier? Or three hours later?"

"Earlier. You need to go to bed."

"Oh, well, all right. Stay safe. Promise me you'll stay safe."

"I will."

"No, promise me."

"I promise."

After I hung up, I sat in my POONG chair, glued to the television until it lulled me back to sleep.

The next morning I got up as the sun was rising and decided to drive by Pinx Video to see if it was still there. In fact, I was curious to see how the whole neighborhood had fared, given what I'd seen on television the night before.

Walking down the stairs to the street, I was happy to find my red, two-door Nissan Sentra still there. No one had stolen it. No one had vandalized it. No one had set it on fire. I opened the big metal gate, got into the boxy, little car and pulled out of the garage—well, perhaps garage is the wrong word; carport with an annoying metal gate was more accurate—then I climbed back out of the car and reclosed the gate. Once on my way, I cut over to Hoover toward Sunset.

I was right about the Circuit City. It was the one on Sunset. That morning it sat there with its windows busted out, giving it a cavernous, gutted look. The merchandise, TVs, VCRs, radios, ghetto-blasters, stereos and car stereos, were all either gone or laying in pieces on the sidewalk in front of the store. But the store hadn't been burned like places in South Central. There they were burning businesses before people had time to finish looting them.

Continuing down Sunset, I saw a sneaker store that had been stripped of its inventory, what might have been a ladies dress shop, and an empty liquor store. None had been burned, though they were *very* damaged.

I turned onto Vermont planning to cut across to Hyperion. The college was untouched, or at least looked untouched from the street. Across from it, though, was the burned out shell of a building. It had been a camera store. A camera store I knew pretty well.

I pulled over to the curb across the street and looked at what had been Guy's Camera. The building had been white with large plate glass windows and a Deco feel. Now, it was a charred shell, windows shattered, roof mostly missing, melted debris littering the floor. Yellow crime scene tape surrounded the building.

I'd taken a photography class from Guy Peterson, the owner. There was an open space at the back of the store where his classes were held, students sat around a table critiquing one another's work. I was a terrible photographer and even worse at critiques, but the class got me out of the house at a time when I needed it. Well, Guy got me out of the house. He was tall with sandy brown hair and soulful eyes. Few of the other people in the class were any more interested in photography than I was.

After the six-week class, amazingly, Guy asked me on a date. Which was wonderful. The date, though, was not. We had an uncomfortable dinner at La Casita Grande—my fault really, it was my first real date after Jeffer died—followed by an awkward encounter at his place. We both promised to call, but neither of us did.

It was terrible to see his business burned to the ground, and somehow awkward. As though our brief acquaintance complicated something that otherwise would have been simple. When people leave our lives we don't truly expect their stories to continue. They should drift off into the distance, rather than suffer very public tragedies.

Pulling away from the curb, I continued down Vermont and wound my way over to Hyperion. I took a deep breath, expecting the worst, but when I got there Pinx Video was untouched. I parked on the street right in front, a rarity. Few people were out, so there was no competition for parking spaces. Keys in hand, I crossed the sidewalk and a few moments later unlocked the front door. Surprisingly, someone had slipped a bag of videos through the night drop. I picked up the plastic bag and brought it over to the counter.

Everything looked in order, so I got on the floor behind the counter and powered up one of the computers. It took forever to come on but that was normal. The store felt very quiet; eerily quiet. When the screen came up, I put in my user ID and password. Then I went to the customer look-up and searched for Peterson, Guy.

We'd gone on one date, so you'd think I might have his number at my apartment, except I knew I didn't. I remembered him giving me his business card with his home number carefully written on the back. After our date, the card floated around in my coin dish for about a week before I threw it away. I didn't feel guilty, since I imagined him doing the same.

His information came up on the computer, so I reached up onto the counter and pulled the desk phone down to where I sat. I felt a little silly. Anybody coming by would think I was terrified—and I wasn't. The streets were quiet and maybe they'd stay that way. Or maybe the National Guard would make it to our neighborhood. Either way, I wasn't feeling frightened just then.

I dialed Guy's number. We had seen each other since the date, of course. He came into Pinx and rented videos. And occasionally I went out to the bars and might see him there. But we never said much more than, "Hello." Which was not a surprise. I had, after all, gotten up and left in the middle of sex. Oh, God, I hoped he wouldn't hate hearing from me. I mean, I was truly sorry about his shop and wanted to say so. I just hoped it didn't add—

His answering machine picked up. I nearly hung up, but then I thought, *Well, this is perfect.* I can leave a message and he doesn't have to call me back if he doesn't want to. And he probably *didn't* want to.

"Hello, Guy, um, this is Noah, Noah Valentine. I know it's been a long time, but I saw what happened to Guy's Camera and just wanted to say how sorry I am. And, I am; really sorry. Really."

That last really made me cringe, so I hung up without leaving my number. Of course, he didn't need my number, he could call me at Pinx. The number was on all the receipts. But I didn't expect him to call back. For one thing, our history, and for another, he obviously had a lot to do just taking care of himself at the moment.

Where was he, though? I wondered. It wasn't unusual not to be home to take a call, except that people were being discouraged from going out. He wasn't at the camera store and he wasn't at home. I was being silly. He was probably with a friend or maybe he had a boyfriend now. There were lots of places he could be that weren't Guy's Camera or his apartment.

I got up off the floor and left, locking the door behind me and hurrying across the sidewalk. It wasn't until I was all the way into my Sentra that I realized something. The ashes that had fallen on us the day before, they were probably from Guy's Camera.

That gave me a sick feeling.

Fifty-three people died, over two thousand were injured, seven thousand fires were set causing one billion dollars in property damage. Rodney King went on the news and asked, "Can we all get along?" and President Bush talked about terror. The Army and Marines arrived in force. After six days it was over.

We reopened Pinx Video on Monday, the fourth of May. Mikey beat me there and set the computers back on the counter where they belonged. He'd stacked up all the returns that had come through the night drop and was slowly going through the process of checking them back in. I went behind the counter and asked of one stack, "These are checked in?"

He nodded, so I took the videos into the storage room and began putting them in their correct slots. For each one, I traded the plastic box for the original cardboard box—with the art and synopsis—that we'd wrapped in clingy plastic so it would last longer. When I got all the plastic boxes back in place, I had a stack of cardboard ones. I took those out to the floor and shelved them in the genres where they belonged. We had a system for that which used stickies. A red sticky meant a video was a new release so it went into one of the three shelves just as you came in. A blue sticky meant the video had been moved to our general library. Those stickies had three letters hand-printed on them to tell us what genre the film belonged in. CLA for classics, HOR for horror, etc.

A half an hour later, we'd checked in and shelved all the videos. Something occurred to me and I asked Mikey, "You didn't charge late fees on any of those, did you?"

"No. We have no way of knowing for sure if they got back on time." They probably didn't, but it wasn't the fault of our customers.

"Good. Don't charge anyone late fees on anything rented before the riots, no matter how long it takes them to bring them back."

"I made a list," Mikey said.

"A list of what?"

"These are the videos that haven't come back," he said, offering me a printed out list. I glanced at it. There weren't a lot. Fifteen customers had not made it in over the weekend to return their movies.

"We should call them," Mikey said. "Let them know we've reopened and we're not charging late fees. But also ask them to bring back the movies."

I glanced at the list and saw something that immediately made me say, "I'll do it."

"Are you sure? I don't—"

Just then our first customer came in. An older woman of about sixty, who I knew had lived in the neighborhood since the nineteen fifties. Our business was returning to normal.

I went back to my little office and called the fifteen names on the list. Most were home. The riots were over, but that didn't mean people were rushing back to work. Guy Peterson's name was on the list. When I dialed his number the answering machine picked up again. I hung up.

Coming out of the office, our one and only customer was telling Mikey that she'd done Gene Tierney's makeup for *The Ghost and Mrs. Muir*.

"You're supposed to think it was England where she lived, but really we were shooting down in Palos Verdes. She was nice. A little daffy, though, I guess. But not as crazy as she got—"

I'd heard that story before, so I waved at Mikey and left the store. I could have interrupted to tell him I was doing errands, but he didn't really care and I was afraid she'd rope me in.

Guy Peterson lived in a two-story, yellow apartment building that looked vaguely Colonial. It was on Los Feliz Boulevard, which was nice if you didn't mind four lanes of traffic as your front yard. There wasn't any parking in front, so I went around the block and found something around the corner.

Guy hadn't moved since our encounter, so I knew which apartment to go to. It was 2F, right in the front. The building's courtyard looked much less Colonial with its brilliant blue pool and plastic-strapped lounge chairs. I ran up the steps to the second floor and knocked on his door. The apartment was a single with one window looking out at the pool and another facing the street.

Before I could knock again, the door opened and out came a tough looking girl, wearing a black Pearl Jam T-shirt and a flannel shirt tied around her waist. She had a tattoo of a hawk on her forearm, made all the more apparent since she had wrapped that arm around a heavy box. I didn't know what to say, but it didn't matter since she thumped right by me as though I wasn't there.

The door hung open, so I went ahead and stepped into the apartment. Inside, was a man in his late fifties with brass colored hair and not much of it. A tubby little woman about the same age tried to disappear next to him. They were obviously packing up Guy's things—but why were they doing that?

Looking up, the man said, "Who are you?"

"Noah. I'm looking for Guy Peterson."

"He's not here."

"Who are you?" I couldn't help asking.

"I'm his father. This is his mother. I imagine you walked right by his sister as you barged in. Who are you to my son?"

"I'm sort of a friend. So, he's not here?"

"He's dead. Got cooked up with that camera store of his."

I was stunned. And not just because Guy was dead. What kind of man says his son 'got cooked up' when he died in a fire? It was coarse, crude, thoughtless. And I had to ignore it.

"Guy was in the store when it burned?" Okay, I just stated the obvious. "Do they know how it happened?"

"Haven't you been watching TV? That's how it happened. Rioters burned the place down and he was in it. Probably had some fool idea he was going to protect the place."

"I'm so sorry. That's so awful."

"Awful for him. We're all still here."

I looked around Guy's apartment. Just as I remembered, there was a full-sized bed, a comfy chair, an old console television with a VCR on top, a desk. There were a couple of boxes of photos—they must have come from a closet, he hadn't kept them sitting out like that—they matched the one Guy's sister had been carrying. I struggled to think of something else to say. Guy hadn't said much about his family on our date. But he did say—

"You're from Fresno?" I asked.

"Yeah."

"I've never been up there. How long a drive is it?"

"Four, five hours. I don't recommend it to sightseers, though. Unless you're partial to hot and ugly."

"I wasn't—I just—it's too bad you had to come so far for something like this."

Guy's sister came back in and said, "Who's this?"

"Friend of your brother's. Valentino or some such."

"Actually, I own Pinx Video." I fumbled to get a card out of my wallet and hand it to Mr. Peterson. "I did know Guy, but I'm really here to get a couple of videos he checked out."

"So you knew he was dead?" his father asked.

"No, no, I didn't."

"You have some kind of pick up service?"

"I saw that the camera shop burned down. And, like I said, I do know Guy. I was in the neighborhood and I thought I'd come by and pick up the videos. You know, to help him out." Is that why I'd come? Or had I come because I started to worry the minute I saw the burned out camera shop? But it hadn't even occurred to me he might have been in there. Oh God—

"Which videos are yours? There's a bunch." He nodded toward a stack of videos sitting on the TV. Mine were the two on top.

"The black case and the brown case. Those are mine."

"Yeah? What are the movies?"

I took the list Mikey had made up out of my pocket and read, "*Silence of the Lambs* and…" I felt my face flush. "…and, uh, *Brothers Should Do It*."

"Luckily Guy didn't have a brother," his father said, then he snorted. I guess he'd been setting me up for the joke.

"How much are you going to give us for them?" Guy's sister asked, stepping between me and the videos.

"Umm, nothing. They're mine. I'm waiving the late fee, I just want them back."

"We're not going to just give them to you. How much are they worth?"

"I have a credit card deposit from your brother. I'll just go back to the store and put it through. If you really want to keep the videos, they're roughly two hundred dollars."

"Give him the videos, Cindy," Guy's father said.

"It doesn't seem fair. He should give us something for them." Limply she handed me the videos.

"Just keep taking those boxes out to the trash. It's almost lunch time," he said. Cindy grabbed a box of photos, hoisted it up to hip level and plodded out of the apartment. They were throwing away Guy's photographs. He'd shown us his work the first day of class. How could they do that? I couldn't believe it. It was like they were just tossing him away.

"Thank you," I couldn't stop myself from saying, though I really didn't think they deserved the courtesy.

As I walked out of the apartment, I heard Guy's mother—who'd been silent the whole time—say, "Doug? When are we going home? I hate this city. It's nothing but niggers and fags."

3

DEATH BRINGS OUT THE WORST IN PEOPLE. NOT THAT I thought Guy's family would be nice people under different circumstances, but I did think they might be less horrible. Jeffer's family, who'd I'd known for years and loved, turned on me in the end. I didn't live with Jeffer for the last six months of his life. I stayed on my friend Robert's sofa for some of that time before getting my own apartment. Jeffer's family had trouble understanding why we were no longer together, and I didn't have the heart to give them a complete explanation.

Before I knew it, before we'd cleaned his things out of what had been and should have remained my house, his family was threatening me. Saying they'd challenge the will on the basis that the loving relationship it described had ended, that I'd moved out and abandoned him to die alone. It wasn't like that; a lot was left out. I couldn't face the prospect of going to court, though, hoping to enforce a will that was a risky proposition under the best of circumstances. We weren't a married couple, after all, and the wrong judge—and there were many wrong judges—the wrong judge could decide I was entitled to none of it. And that would mean I'd be left with nothing more than legal fees and memories.

So I made a deal with them. I kept the video store—which

Jeffer was minimally involved in, anyway—and split the proceeds from the sale of the house. That left me with an income and a rainy day lump of cash.

Of course there were things in the house I'd wanted. Things that were mine, things that were ours. A particular chair, a lamp, a picture, a photograph album that was mostly me and my family. At the last minute they wouldn't let me have them. So I spent nearly a week driving through the alley behind the house to see what they might have thrown away and finding a fair number of treasures.

I was standing next to the Sentra about to get in as I thought that. Then I looked down the street and about a hundred feet away, there was the alley behind Guy's building. Getting into my car, I tossed the videos onto the passenger seat, started the engine and pulled a quick U-ie. When I got to the end of the alley, I slowed. I didn't want Guy's sister to see what I was about to do. She wasn't there, though, so I zipped down the alley.

Guy's building was halfway down. When I was right next to the green metal dumpster for his building, I parked. Sitting on the ground next to it were the two boxes of photos Cindy had carried out. It looked like she was trying to save herself the energy of actually tossing them into the bin.

I jumped out of the Sentra, opened the trunk and quickly loaded in the two boxes. There was at least one more box in the apartment. I wondered if I should drive around the block a few times to see if Cindy would bring it out, but just then she came out into the alley carrying the third box. I slammed my trunk shut. The look on her face said she wasn't likely to give me that box any time soon.

I walked around and started to climb into the car.

"Hey, that's stealing," she said, grabbing the driver's door.

"No, it's garbage picking. That's something else entirely." I grabbed the door away from her and shut it.

"I'm going to call the police," she yelled.

"Go ahead!" I yelled back. And then pulled away.

I wasn't afraid she'd call the police. For one thing, I was sure the LAPD was still overwhelmed. Yes, the riot was over. No, they had not solved all the crimes connected with it. I really doubted they'd come out if she complained I'd stolen something she'd thrown away.

As I drove back to Pinx, I was exhilarated. I had no idea what I'd do with the two boxes of photos. I didn't even know if any of them were his "good" photos. I just knew it was wrong to throw so much of Guy's life away. The photos were his life's work and I had to save them. Oh, hell, maybe it had something to do with having lost so much of my own life. Whatever.

Parking in back of the store, I went in through the back door. The door we discouraged customers from using by putting up a sign that said EMPLOYEES ONLY. Customers still came through it, just not as many.

It was slow that day. Mondays typically were slow, but that Monday was especially dead—poor choice of words, sorry. We weren't busy and I was surprised. I thought people might still want to stay close to home and watch a movie or two.

I decided to leave around six. Mikey had already left at four, and Carl and Denny had come in at three. They were an older couple, semi-retired, who insisted they work the same shift. I didn't really need two people on a Monday night, but they wanted Fridays and Saturdays off so I went along with it. The two of them together equaled one great employee, just twice as expensive. Before I left, I told them they could close at nine if they wanted to. I figured they wouldn't. They had each other to talk to, so they didn't care if the place was empty.

When I got back to my apartment, I opened the gate, pulled into the garage and popped the trunk. I took out Guy's two boxes and set them aside so I could reclose the gate. It was an annoying process but car theft in the neighborhood was common and the metal gate provided a bit of a deterrent.

I climbed up to the courtyard juggling the boxes. Louis and Marc were already seated at the table on the patio. Marc had changed out of his "studio" drag into a pair of shorts and a Hawaiian shirt. Louis wore an apron that said, "Fellate the

Host." I think he had it made somewhere. His personal version of "Kiss the Cook."

"Noah! Come have dinner with us," Louis called out. I was already heading over—I really needed a glass of wine—when he added, "Leon is coming."

Well, I couldn't just stop, so I kept on. Leon was a friend of theirs who I wouldn't mind so much if I didn't sometimes have the feeling they were trying to fix us up.

"What on earth are you carrying?" Marc asked. He was smoking a recently lit cigarette. Louis didn't smoke and wouldn't let Marc smoke in the apartment—a big part of why they were almost always outside.

I set the boxes down on the ground by the table.

"Do you know the camera store? The one on Vermont?"

"Guy's Camera?" Louis asked.

"Yes."

"Wait, who?" Marc wanted to know.

"Guy the Camera Guy. We talked to him one time at the Griffs. Tall, sexy as hell."

"Everyone we talk to at the Griffs is tall and sexy as hell," Marc said, then added for my benefit, "It's like a rule. We can't talk to anyone less attractive than we are."

"He's dead," I said flatly.

"Oh, my," said Marc.

There was an empty wine glass on the table, presumably for Leon. Louis filled it and moved it in front of me.

"What happened?" he asked.

"The second day of the riots, his store burned down with him in it. He must have thought he could protect it."

I was very glad I hadn't taken Mikey's advice and attempted to protect my store. Yes, nothing had happened to Pinx, but if I'd been there, moving around, taunting the rioters, maybe it would have. You never know.

"That seems so odd," Marc said.

"What seems odd?" I asked.

"I hope this doesn't sound racist, but the blacks in South Central were burning businesses down. They were angry. Are angry. They don't feel like they got justice so they're striking out. And honestly I can't blame them. The LAPD is hideous." He stubbed out his cigarette in a glass ashtray. "But it's different up here. Most of the rioters in Silver Lake were Hispanic. They're angry, too, but not because of the police, not because they didn't get justice. They're angry because they're poor. It's more about money than race for them. That's why they didn't burn down as many buildings."

I thought about what I'd seen on TV. Hispanic-looking people stealing TVs from Circuit City and sneakers from a shoe store. These were things they wanted but couldn't afford. So why did they loot the camera store? Did they want cameras?

Louis popped back into the apartment.

"Do you really think poor people want high-end cameras?" I asked.

"To sell, sure. But why burn the building? That's my point." He shrugged in an exaggerated way. He was right. There wasn't a good answer. But then was there a good answer to any of it?

Louis came back out with a tray of cheese and crackers. "They got Frederick's of Hollywood," he said with a smirk.

"Burned?" I asked.

"No, just looted. But can you imagine? 'Honey I'm home from the riots. I got you some crotchless panties.'"

He started chuckling. I had to laugh, too. People stealing lingerie in the middle of a riot. What were they thinking? Maybe it wasn't so strange that the camera store burned.

"What's in the boxes?" Marc asked.

"Guy's photographs."

"What are you doing with them?"

"His family is cleaning out his apartment—"

"Already? Talk about not letting the body get cold."

"Anyway, they were throwing them out and I just—it seemed wrong."

Then I remembered something, well, part of something. On our date, guy had talked about how much he loved photography. How much it meant to him. He said he loved it more than any man he'd ever—

29

"What?" Louis had been asking me something.

"How did you know Guy?" he repeated.

"I took his class."

"Oh, yeah. I know a lot of people who took that class," Louis said. "Some of them were even interested in photography."

"Well, let's see what's in there," Marc said. I lifted the first box up to the table. Reaching in, I grabbed a short stack of prints and handed them to Marc, then took some for myself.

"Do you want some, Louis?"

"Sure, why not?"

I gave him a stack, as well. Pulling the photos out of the box, I realized the bottom of the box was lined with film canisters, presumably holding negatives.

Beginning to go through the pictures in front of me, I immediately saw that they were in a wide range of styles. That made sense since his class covered portraiture, landscapes and journalism as distinct branches of photography. I remembered him bringing in samples of each.

My stack was mostly landscapes: Joshua Tree, Big Bear, random places in between. The shots were good, though probably not good enough to hang. Gradually they shifted over to cityscapes: Palm Springs, West Hollywood, Silver Lake at night.

"I think these are from the AB101 protest," Louis said. He laid out some black-and-white shots of crowds taken at night.

"Those were so much fun," Marc said. The previous fall we'd taken to the streets when the governor refused to sign a bill protecting gay rights.

"I don't know that I'd call them fun," I said. "Exhilarating, empowering, exciting, important—"

"All Marc really remembers is that we went with a flask of martinis," Louis said.

"No, that isn't it at all. I happen to think it's fun to do important, empowering things." Then he said, "Oh my. Look at this."

He laid a photo out on the table. Right away I saw that it was unlike the rest. There were five men wearing boy's Scoutingtype clothing, blue uniforms with shorts and kerchiefs. They were kicking a man who was cowering naked in front of them. Around the edges of the frame were policemen holding batons. Behind the policemen, a giant tree hanging over them. It was a night shot, though carefully lit. Obviously, it was some kind of commentary on the King beating. What it meant exactly escaped me.

"Weird, but kind of powerful," I said.

"I know. I feel like it's supposed to mean something that I'm not really understanding," Marc said.

"He obviously doesn't like the LAPD," Louis said.

"Who does?"

"What are those uniforms?" Marc asked. "If they're supposed to be Boy Scouts they're all wrong. I was an Eagle Scout."

"They're Frontier Scouts. More conservative than Boy Scouts," Louis explained.

"More conservative than Boy Scouts? I didn't know that was possible."

"Where would he get all those uniforms?" I asked. People to photograph were not a problem in L.A., costuming them could be.

"He's into uniforms, it's his thing," Louis said.

"How do you know that?"

"Yes, dear, how *do* you know that?"

"Don't you remember, Marc? He was wearing a uniform that time we talked to him. I think he's in some uniform fetish group."

"Which was he wearing?" I asked. "LAPD or Frontier Scout?"

"Sheriff, I think. It was tan."

"There's something familiar about those photos," Marc said. "I feel like I've seem them before."

"They're a little Mapplethorpe-ian," Louis suggested.

"I don't think that's a word."

"It is now."

"Is that legal?" I asked. "To wear a policeman's uniform?"

"It's probably fine as long as you don't arrest anyone." Louis guessed. "Mmmm-hmmmm. I think I hit the jackpot. My stack is mostly artistic male nudes." He finger-quoted artistic.

"Oh, let me see," Marc said."

"When I'm finished."

Just then, Leon came up the stairs from the street. He was nearly forty, dyed his hair white-blond and wore a dark blue business suit. He'd opened his jacket but hadn't bothered taking it off. It was in the low seventies and windy, which might have mattered if we weren't sitting beneath a twelve-foot tall bird of paradise.

"What is all this?" Leon asked.

"You know the camera shop on Vermont?" Marc asked in return.

"Across from the college?"

"Yes, that one. Well it burned down with the guy who owns it inside."

"Last Thursday," I added.

"Noah stole these from the family."

"I didn't steal them. They left them in the alley."

"So you stole them," Leon teased.

"You can't steal garbage. And when you leave something by the dumpster in the alley, that's what it is. Garbage."

Louis stood up. "Here, look at the artistic nudes while I get you a drink."

Leon took the stack but didn't look through it. "Oh God! It was a terrible day at work. Everyone was all out of sorts." He did something with international film sales, I never figured out exactly what. "I have seven women working for me. I have a Korean girl who's convinced the black girls want to kill her. The Latina hates immigrants so she blames everything on them. The black girls feel like people are blaming the riot on them, which is ridiculous. One of them is married to a plastic surgeon and lives in Brentwood for God's sake. And the three white women are so busy trying not to offend anyone they won't say a word."

Louis returned with a martini for Leon. "Thank you. However did you know?"

"It was the panic and dread in your eyes."

"You say the sweetest things." He guzzled half his martini. "So, why did you steal Guy's photos?"

"Stop saying steal," I said. "I rescued them."

"Are they that good?"

"They're okay."

"Okay? You've saved mediocre photographs for posterity. How lovely."

Louis had gone back to looking through his pile. "Hello. I think we have a winner here." He kept flipping through. "Oh, definitely."

He spread about ten pictures out on the table. They were all of an attractive young man in his early twenties. The poses were provocative. In most of them he held a very impressive, very erect penis in his hand. Sometimes he used two hands.

"Oh my," said Marc.

"At least he finishes what he starts," Louis said, pointing at the most *explosive* of the photos.

"I know him," said Leon.

"You do?" Louis raised an eyebrow.

"He's a VJ. Has a show on that new music channel, Video Hits. Very popular." Pointing at his obvious assets, he said, "And now we know why."

4

WHEN I GOT TO PINX VIDEO THE NEXT MORNING, THERE were two policemen waiting for me. I didn't notice them when I walked in. Yes, there were two guys in their thirties skulking around the classic films section, but that didn't seem unusual. With a porn section like ours it was common for men to skulk around the store for a while before slipping back into the adult section, usually the minute we looked away.

"I think we should change out the posters today," I told Mikey when I got to the counter. "Time for a fresh start."

The studios sent us new posters every week or so. The big videos coming out soon were *The Prince of Tides*, *Cape Fear* and *The Addams Family*. We needed to get them in the window soon to generate excitement.

"Those two guys are here for you. They're LAPD," Mikey said. Then under his breath he whispered, "What did you do?" The look on his face told me he didn't think I was interesting enough to break the law.

I came out from behind the counter and walked over to the classics section. "Can I help you gentlemen? I'm Noah Valentine."

The shorter one was bedraggled and blond, his face the map of a hard life. He reminded me of Charles Bronson, just not as friendly. The taller one was better looking, with honeyed skin and coal black hair.

The shorter one said, "Nino Percy. Murder squad out of Rampart Station."

"Javier O'Shea. Same." I had the immediate feeling Javier's family reunions were interesting in at least two languages.

"What can I do for you?" I asked. "I'm guessing you're not here to rent videos."

"I understand you saw the Peterson family yesterday?" Percy said more than asked.

"I did."

"You're a friend of Guy's?"

"Not exactly. He had some videos checked out. They were overdue and I knew his business had burned down, so I stopped by to pick up the videos and tell him there were no late fees because of the riot."

"Really? You stopped by to personally pick up videos?" Percy said with a lot of derision. Though I had to admit, it did sound suspicious.

O'Shea took over. "Did you know Peterson socially? Or was he just a customer?"

"I took his photography class about a year ago. We had dinner once." My cheeks flushed, suggesting more.

"Do you know any of his friends?" Percy asked.

"No. I don't remember him talking about his friends. I'm sure he had friends. He just didn't say anything to me about them."

Percy stared at me as though I were lying.

"Why is this important? I assumed...wasn't Guy killed in the riot?"

"That's the way it appears, yes," O'Shea said. "We just want to talk to some of his friends. Get an idea what his mind set was that night."

"Afternoon," I corrected. "The fire was in the afternoon."

"Why do you say that?"

"Well, I live a few blocks from the camera store. We were in the courtyard having lunch when ashes began to fall. I suppose they could have come from somewhere else, I just thought…"

"Well," said O'Shea. "If you run across any of his friends ask them to call us."

"You must be very busy," I said. "A lot of people died."

"We're always busy," said Percy, and turned to stalk out of the store. O'Shea briefly looked at me and then followed.

They left me with a very unsettled feeling. Was Guy's death more complicated than it seemed? I didn't have a good way to answer that question, unless—

I went back to Mikey at the counter and said, "I need to run an errand."

"You know, we should talk to a lawyer before we give the police any information on our customers."

"What brought that up?" I asked.

"Those two policeman. They were asking about a customer right? I mean, they weren't here to talk to you about you, were they?"

"I'm perfectly capable of breaking the law," I said in my defense.

"No you're not. You're not the type."

I decided to ignore the paradoxical insult. "They were asking questions about Guy Peterson."

"Oh, him. He owns that camera store on Vermont."

"Yes. The one that burned down. With him in it."

He gave me a funny look. "Did you know that when you went to pick up videos up from him?"

"How did you—?"

"You went to run an errand and you came back with the videos he'd rented. Two and two usually equals four." Sometimes it felt like Mikey knew more about me than I knew myself.

"No, I didn't know he was dead. His family gave me the videos. But not before they tried to sell them to me."

"That's sad, that he's dead. And that he had an awful family, I guess. He was always friendly when he came in."

"I don't want to say I told you so—" Well, I kind of did.

"But you see it would have been a bad idea to stay and try to protect the store."

"Of course, I see that," he said. "You didn't have a gun. It would have been foolish to try and protect the store without at least one gun. Three would have been optimal."

I had no idea why Mikey thought he knew about guns and I didn't want to know. Of course, I didn't think Guy Peterson had a gun. At least, no one had mentioned a gun being found. Did he have one? Had it been taken by the rioters? For all I knew he might have been shot before the store was burned. I'd assumed the fire was what killed him, but was that even true? I should have asked the police more questions. Not that they would have answered them. But I could have asked.

"How's Randy? Have things calmed down at the hospital?"

"He's back down to ten hour shifts. No days off, though. They're still over-crowded. All elective surgeries have been rescheduled."

"Well, I have something I need to do," I said.

"What kind of something?" Mikey pried.

"Just something. Why don't you put up the new posters while I'm gone. And take down whatever…"

His eyes lit up. He had very specific ideas about poster placement that I rarely let him implement.

Ten minutes later, I was parking in front of what was left of Guy's Camera. I got out and walked up to the burned out store. The crime scene tape was still up, fluttering in the breeze.

I looked around, God knows for what, and stepped over the tape—which clearly said DO NOT CROSS. The double front door to the shop had been two large pieces of glass framed in varnished wood. The glass was gone and I was able to step through into the shop. It had been a while, but I tried to remember what the space had once looked like.

The front of the store had been devoted to tables and shelves which held the cameras Guy was selling. I thought that a terrible idea. Someone could just step into the shop and grab a camera. By the time Guy got to the front door the thief would be long gone. I stood in the front for a moment. The tables were still standing, on them cameras that had warped and melted. On the wall, there had been shelves. The shelves had either fallen in the heat or had been scraped off the wall by firemen. There on the floor were dozens of cameras, smashed, charred, destroyed.

In the back of the store, there had been an open area with a large worktable on one side. The cash register—melted like something out of Dali—and a darkroom were on the other side. The worktable was in blackened pieces. It was obvious the fire had burned hotter and longer in the back than it had in the front. I wondered if that meant something.

Looking at the surrealistic cash register, I wondered if there was anything in the drawer. At Pinx, we locked the cash drawer in the desk in my office. But that was mainly done so that employees couldn't steal. Certainly, if someone were to rob the store they could make their way back to the office easily. But I didn't think Guy had employees. And I didn't remember anyplace where he could have hidden a cash drawer.

I decided to try and open the drawer. The cash register was from sometime in the eighties and really wasn't much more than a plastic adding machine on top of a metal cash drawer. The keys were all melted so even if I could turn it on, I wouldn't be able to get the drawer to open automatically. I looked around to find something to pry the drawer open with.

It took a bit, but I finally found something on the floor in front of the door to the burned out dark room. It was some kind of specialized tool made of four pieces of metal crossed over each other, like a frame for playing tic-tac-toe. Two of the metal pieces had a screwdriver tip on one end and a kind of awl on the other. The tool was sticky and black with soot.

I stuck one of the screwdriver tips into the lock and tried to force the drawer open. Just then someone behind me said, "What are you doing in here?"

The voice belonged to a man of about seventy. He was thin, pale, and swayed to his right. I turned around and faced him. "I was a friend of Guy's," was the only thing I could think to say, though it was hardly an answer. Or even true.

"Nobody's supposed to be in here."

"And you are...?"

"I own this building. Sherman Dooley." He was eyeing the sooty tool in my hand.

"I'm sorry you lost your building, Mr. Dooley," I said carefully.

He shrugged. "It's going to be a month before I can get anyone to come clean up this mess."

"Yes, well, there were a lot of fires."

"Of course there were a lot of fires."

"I know. I'm sorry for your loss," I said again.

"It's not the end of the world," he said. Of course, it was the end of the world for Guy Peterson. But Dooley didn't seem to care about that.

"What are you doing there?" he finally asked.

"Trying to open the cash drawer."

"If there's anything in there it's mine."

"Okay. I wasn't trying to open it to get the money. I just wanted to see if there was money in there."

"So you just like to look at it?" he asked, obviously doubtful.

"No. It's just—most of the cameras are still here. If the money's still here, too, then maybe the shop wasn't looted."

"What are you saying?"

"I don't know exactly. I'm just wondering if maybe the building wasn't set on fire because of the riot."

"Are you accusing me of something?"

"What? No." Of course, I immediately wondered if I should be accusing him of something. I turned back to the cash register and jammed the screw end of the tool I was holding into the lock and gave it a good hard turn. I felt it break but the drawer didn't budge. I twisted until the edge of the drawer pulled away from its casing. Then I slipped the screw end into the slot and pried until the drawer finally popped out. It was full. Twenties, tens, fives, ones and change. Though I imagined it smelled of smoke, the money was intact.

Dooley stepped forward and began to fill his pockets.

"Did you know Guy?" I asked.

"He was always five days late with the rent." It was pretty clear where Dooley's priorities lay.

"So you wouldn't have any idea why he was here that day?"

"He was protecting his investment like they did in Koreatown."

"So you think he had a gun?"

"I don't know."

"Do you know what time the fire started?"

"I got a phone call about it near four o'clock. The whole place was gone by the time I got down here."

"And they knew Guy was inside?"

"Well sure. They was in here chopping things up. He lay right where you're standing," Dooley said.

I moved instinctively and looked down at the floor. It was badly charred in a way that the front of the store wasn't. I realized I was still holding the tool I'd used to open the drawer.

I set it down on the counter. Glancing at my hand, I noticed something brown across my palm. That didn't seem right. Soot was black or gray maybe. Not brown. I looked closely at the tool. The sharp awl like tips were covered in something sticky and brown but what—

Casually, I picked up the tool again. I said good-bye to Mr. Dooley, but he was too busy trying to pry up a quarter that had stuck to the plastic drawer to notice me leaving. Or to notice I'd taken the tool with me.

"Tell me if I'm crazy," I said that night in the courtyard after I'd explained everything that had happened that day. I'd stayed at the store until almost nine, feeling guilty for having spent time away looking at Guy's store. So, I arrived home in time for dessert with Louis, Marc and their friend, Leon. Louis had made flourless chocolate cake that he'd served with fresh whipped cream and Irish coffee. "I went back to Guy's shop and noticed there were a lot of cameras, most of them melted, still in the shop. There was cash in the cash register. And there was this."

I put the tool out onto the table.

"Do you guys know what it is?"

Marc and Louis looked at me blankly, while Leon said, "It's a spanner wrench. You use it to repair camera lenses."

"How do you know that?" Marc asked.

"I went to film school. And, believe it or not, they actually taught us things." He picked it up and pointed to the four adjustable knobs. "See, you can turn these and make it whatever size—oh, there's something sticky all over it. What is that?" He sniffed at his fingers and said, "Oooo, Louis smell this."

He stuck his fingers under Louis' nose. Louis pushed back in his chair. "Uh no. 'Oooo, Louis smell this' is never a good recommendation."

"Just smell."

Louis did. "Is that blood?"

"I think so," Leon said. "I mean, it smells like something a butcher left out on the counter."

Louis looked at me and asked, "Do you think this is the murder weapon? One of the rioters picked this up and stabbed Guy with it before the place was torched?"

"I don't know," I admitted. "It might be."

"You should turn it over to the police," Marc said.

"But...what if it wasn't a rioter? What if it was someone just using the riot as cover? Is that crazy?"

"Absolutely. Isn't there some rule that the most likely explanation is actually the explanation?" Louis said before refilling our coffee.

"Occam's razor; and that's not exactly what it says. I think Noah's onto something, though. Especially since the police are poking around," Leon disagreed.

"They're just doing their jobs. Do you take cream, Noah? I forget."

"Are they, though?" Leon continued. "Fifty-some people died, thousands injured. It sounds like they have a lot of jobs to do. Why investigate this death if it's just random mob violence?"

"That does seem suspicious," I said.

"Let's not get carried away," Marc said. "If Guy the Camera Guy was killed by random rioters, how would that have happened?"

We all took a moment, sipped our coffee, took a bite of cake and thought about our answer.

"Given what we all saw on TV, looters would have broken the front windows and started taking things," I said.

"And Guy the Camera Guy would have tried to stop them," Leon picked up. "Possibly getting stabbed with the spanner wrench and then trapped in a burning building."

"Except there's no evidence of looting, according to Noah."

"And Guy the Cam—Guy died at the back of the store. Which was also where the fire was most intense."

"All right, let's say there were no looters," Marc suggested. "That doesn't mean people weren't going around torching buildings. It was a riot. No one handed out instructions."

"They just randomly chose that building? And he happened to be inside bleeding on a spanner wrench?' Leon asked, before telling Louis, "Darling I'll take more coffee but make mine whiskey with a splash of coffee."

"Okay, first of all, it was the only building for blocks that burned. And second of all, if they did randomly torch that building, wouldn't he have tried to get things out of there? It didn't look like anything had been moved and the cash register was still in there full of cash."

"I don't think you're crazy," Leon said. "I think he was murdered."

"Yeah, I think you're right," Louis agreed.

"What do the police think?" Marc asked.

"I don't know. They mainly wanted to know who his friends were."

"Well, if he was murdered, it might be a friend who did it," Marc guessed.

"Or his friends might know."

"All right then," Louis said. "If he was murdered, who do we think did it?"

"Well obviously, it's the police," Leon said. "Why else would they be poking around?"

"But why would the police want to kill him?" Marc asked.

Louis asked. "Those pictures with the Frontier Scouts aren't flattering."

"They're also not real," Marc pointed out.

"We'll have to look at them again," I said. The photos were upstairs, though, and the cake was too tempting and the Irish coffee too strong to be interrupted.

"Well if it's about photos, then I'm switching my vote to Rex Hoffman," Leon said.

"Who's that?" I asked.

"The VJ with the hidden assets."

"No, you're wrong," insisted Louis. "You have to follow the money. The person who'll benefit the most here is the landlord. He'll get a nice fat insurance check, then he'll sell the property for what he would have gotten even before the fire."

"He was at least seventy," I pointed out.

"The murder weapon isn't exactly heavy. Neither are matches."

"What about the family?" Marc asked. "They sound horrible."

"I think they were in Fresno when Guy was murdered."

"Well, that's hardly an airtight alibi. Do you think they'll get a lot of money? Do you think he had life insurance?"

"I don't think he was rich. And I doubt he had life insurance. The inventory in the camera shop was probably insured, though."

"We need more information," Leon said. Then he turned to me and asked, "Do you want to talk to Rex Hoffman?"

"Me? Um, yeah, yes, I would like to talk to Rex Hoffman."

"Come by the studio tomorrow about eleven. I'll leave a drive-on for you."

"Oh, I don't want you to get into trouble."

"I won't get into trouble. I'm not going to use my name. I'll look through the directory and find someone in the production company that makes Rex's show. I'll say that's who I am."

"Is that all there is to it?"

"Well, not exactly. The guard will direct you to the sound-stage where they shoot Rex's show. There will be some trailers outside. One of them will have Rex's name written on a piece of masking tape stuck to the door. Just knock and Rex will answer."

"What if he's not there?"

"Then just go inside and wait. They never lock those things."

"Why is he going to tell me anything?" I asked.

"Because you're going to give him the photographs."

5

Paramount, where Leon worked, was only a few blocks away from my apartment with its main entrance on Melrose. I was to get there just before noon. I'd called Mikey and told him I'd come into the video store a few hours later. I dressed in my most business-like clothing: a pair of khakis, a button down shirt and a tie that was a bit too formal for either —the only one I had. Well, that's not true, I did have a black bowtie from when I worked as a waiter, but that wouldn't have worked either. Not to mention a black suit I swore I'd never wear again.

I'd bought a nine by twelve manila envelope at Office Depot and put Guy's photos of Rex inside along with the negatives.

Leon had wanted to hold out one of the photos for himself, saying, "It's for my collection."

"You have a collection of famous people ejaculating?"

"Maybe."

I held my ground and wouldn't give Leon any of the shots. If I was going to give Rex back the photos, then I was going to give him back *all* the photos.

When I pulled into the ornate double gate, there were two cars in front of me. The marine layer was in full effect, a thick layer of clouds forming each morning that kept the temperature

47

in the mid-sixties. We might see some sun in the afternoon when the clouds burned off, but there was no guarantee.

The first car was allowed onto the lot and we pulled forward. My palms started to sweat and I wiped them on my khakis one at a time. This was stupid, I thought. I should back up and leave. Except, I couldn't. There was a black BMW behind me.

What was the worst thing that could happen? The guard would tell me I couldn't come on the lot. It would be embarrassing, but that would be it. And the worst thing Rex Hoffman could do to me was have me thrown off the lot. I could survive that. No big deal.

Why was I bothering, though? Why was I risking anything, even embarrassment, for someone I barely knew? The only answer I could think of, and it came to me rather quickly, was that no one else was. I think if I could believe that someone else was going to try to find out what happened to Guy, I'd stop.

The next car pulled onto the lot and it was my turn. I pulled forward. The guard was black and middle-aged. I smiled at him, but he didn't smile back.

"I'm Noah Valentine. There should be a drive-on for me."

The guard looked at a clipboard he was holding. Almost immediately he said, "There's no Valentine. Who was supposed to call it in?"

That wasn't good. I couldn't give him Leon's name. Actually, I didn't even know his last name, so if I wanted to I couldn't.

"You know, they're really busy, could you just look again?"

It annoyed him, but he did it anyway. As he looked down the list his expression changed and he said, "Hmmm…" Looking in at me he said, "Nora Balentine?"

"Yeah, that's probably it." I wondered if Leon had done that to me deliberately.

"Okay. Visitor parking is straight ahead. You're going to stage eleven, which is across from the Crosby Building on Avenue L."

None of that made sense to me, but it didn't matter. I was

getting onto the lot. If it took all day to find Rex Hoffman, then it took all day.

I found a place to park, got out of the car, and, of course, I walked off in the wrong direction. But the stages—which were all about four stories tall and came in various sizes—had gigantic numbers painted on them. So when I found myself standing in front of Stage 14, I knew I'd made a wrong turn, or hadn't made a turn at all.

Since I didn't have cable, I knew almost nothing about Rex Hoffman's show *Countdown Four-Oh!* other than he spent two hours introducing the top forty videos.

I walked past the Zukor building. Stage 12 was on my left and Stage 7 directly in front of me. I took a left turn. As I walked, I tried to think of the earliest Paramount film we had at Pinx. I was pretty sure we had a copy of *Wings*, which I thought might be from that studio. That and *Napoleon* were our only silent films.

Stage 11 was coming up on my left. Just as Leon had told me, there were a couple of small travel trailers sitting across the street in front of the Crosby building. The second trailer I looked at had a piece of masking tape stuck next to the door that read, REX HOFFMAN, in blue marker.

I took a deep breath and knocked on the door. There was no answer. Following Leon's suggestion, I tried the door. It opened so I walked in. I stood just inside the door waiting for someone to run up and scream at me for letting myself in, but then I realized if anyone had noticed me entering the trailer they might assume someone inside had yelled, "Come in."

It was a standard travel trailer, except there was a case of Evian on the counter, next to a portable TV/VCR combo and a boom box with a CD player. There were CDs and videocassettes everywhere on the dinette table mixed in with newspapers, trade papers and magazines.

The newspaper on top had an article about the riots. Skimming through I saw that it included numbers similar to ones I'd seen before: 58 people were listed as dead, more than 2,000 injured, and nearly 200 missing. It broke the numbers down further: who was white, who was black, who was Latino. None of the dead were policemen. The article went on to talk about how the police were seen abandoning whole neighborhoods to the rioters. Which explained—

"Well. Hello?"

I looked up and there was Rex Hoffman. He looked different with his clothes on, smaller somehow and, of course, not as "friendly." He was also noticeably older.

"The door was open, so I came in to wait."

"You shouldn't just barge into people's trailers. It could be taken the wrong way."

"You could have locked the door."

He ignored that. "So, who are you?"

"My name is Noah Valentine. I am, or was, a friend of Guy Peterson. I brought some pictures—"

"Oh. I see. Look, as I explained to Gary—"

"Guy."

"Whatever. I don't pay blackmail. If you bought those pictures hoping to make a killing you've been conned."

"Guy was blackmailing you?" I asked, surprised.

"No. He was *trying* to blackmail me. There's a difference. I said, 'Go ahead, publish the photos if you want. I'll just explain that I was young and stupid and broke. If Vanessa Williams can live down her nude photos, I can live down mine.'"

"How long ago was this?"

"A couple of weeks, I guess. A month? Out of curiosity, how much did you pay for the pictures?"

"I didn't pay for them. Guy died."

"Well. I would shed a tear, but I'm not that good an actor." He looked me over. "So, if you're not here to blackmail me, then why are you here?"

To find out if he'd murdered Guy was the answer, but I could hardly say that. "I want to give you the pictures and in return I'm hoping you'll answer a few questions."

"Answer a few questions? You are blackmailing me, aren't you? Just not for money."

"I don't really see it that way," I said.

"Well, no, you probably wouldn't. What do you want to know?"

"Why did Guy have the pictures in the first place?"

"I told you. I was young and stupid and broke."

"Guy didn't have other photos like that." There were nudes, but none as explicit as the ones with Rex. Of course, there was that whole other box his sister wouldn't give me, so I was making an assumption.

"I don't know what he did or didn't do with other models."

"And they were never published." If they'd been published Guy would never have tried to blackmail Rex since there would be hundreds, even thousands of copies.

"No, they weren't."

"Guy wasn't in that business, was he?"

"All right, fine. We were together for a while and just took the pictures for fun one day. I should have asked for them when we broke up, but I wasn't exactly thinking ahead. Is that all you want to know?"

"When did you become a VJ?"

"Two years ago."

I nodded. "How much money did Guy ask for?"

"Why does that matter?"

"If he was just greedy he'd have come to you as soon as you showed up on TV. So, he must have needed the money for something specific. Maybe he was just asking for what he needed."

"And maybe he just woke up one day and decided to be a scumbag."

"Yeah, maybe."

"He wanted thirty thousand."

"Did he say why he wanted the money?"

"Blackmailers don't explain themselves."

"But, you were friends once."

"Sure. He said he was in a little trouble and needed money. I didn't care to know more."

"So you said no on principle?"

"Not just principle. Video Hits is kind of a new channel.

This job pays scale. It's an okay living, but I don't have wads of cash lying around, you know?"

Something was getting clearer for me. Guy could have outed Rex. He could have admitted their relationship and used the photos as proof. Maybe he wasn't quite as bad as Rex thought he was. Or maybe he was planning to blackmail Rex in stages.

"Have I answered all your questions?"

"Where were you last Thursday afternoon?"

"During the riots? At home with the door locked and the shades drawn."

"Can you prove that?"

"I made a couple of long distance calls. I didn't want people to worry about me."

"People?" I asked.

"My sister mainly." He blushed as though talking to his family was the worst thing he'd admitted. Of course, he could be lying about that. It would take weeks to get a copy of his phone bill—if he was even willing to show it to me when it arrived.

I was out of questions. I pushed the envelope across the dinette toward him. "I found the negatives. They're in there, as well."

"Thank you."

"Well, I should let you get back to work."

"I'm on break. Would you like to give me a blow job?"

"Oh, um, well, thank you for offering. But, no."

Years ago, before Jeffer, I might have taken him up on the offer. But things were different now. There were a lot of reasons not to have sex with him, not the least of which was that he might be a murderer.

Marc and Louis were spending the evening watching a four-hour opera at the Dorothy Chandler, so they weren't in the courtyard when I got home. I had promised to call Leon, though, so when I got into my apartment I poured myself a glass of chardonnay, put on a Chet Baker CD, and sat down at my desk. For a moment, I sipped the wine and looked out at the city at night. The lights were sparkling again and it gave me the eerie feeling that nothing had happened; that people hadn't been killed, that buildings hadn't been burned. I called the number Leon had given me.

"Ye-ays?" he answered.

"Leon, it's Noah. I saw Rex Hoffman."

"You did. Wonderful. And no one threw you off the lot?"

"No. He didn't even ask me how I got onto the lot."

"So what did you find out? Do you think he killed your friend?"

"I'm not ready to take him off the list yet, but I think it's less likely."

"Hmmm…did you find out anything interesting?"

"Yes. Guy was trying to blackmail him."

"Really?"

"He thought that's what I was there to do."

"Well, you do look like a blackmailer."

"Very funny. The thing is, I think Guy needed money for something."

"You don't think he might just have been greedy?"

"If he was just greedy, why wait? Rex has been on TV for a couple of years."

"What do you think he needed money for?"

"I don't know. He asked for thirty thousand dollars."

"Down payment on a condo? Or maybe a brand new BMW?"

"No, I think it's something more immediate. If he wanted a car he could have gone to Rex sooner. This is something he needed thirty thousand for now."

"Like he needed surgery?"

"Or someone else did."

"Hmmm. Did you give Rex a blow job?"

"What? No? Why would you—"

"Relax. Rex is famous for that. That's half the reason I got you onto the lot, so you'd tell me all about it."

"I said, no."

"Well, that's boring."

"Sorry. I didn't know I was this evening's entertainment."

"You know Marc and Louis are dying of curiosity. You never bring anyone home. You don't even stay out late. They've decided the real mystery here is your sex life."

This was very uncomfortable. I didn't want to discuss this with anyone, no less Leon Whose-Last-Name-I-Didn't-Even-Know.

"Well, I have to go. But, um, by the way, at the gate they were expecting Nora Balentine. That wasn't deliberate, was it?"

"What? Moi?"

6

MARLENE DIETRICH DIED—IN GERMANY SOMEWHERE, and it had nothing to do with the riots. I spent most of Thursday morning creating a special shelf for her videos. We'd noticed an uptick in the rentals of our classics when an actor died—especially the ones from the studio days—so we tried to encourage those rentals.

We had my two favorites, *Witness for the Prosecution* and *Stage Fright*; *Destry Rides Again*; *Judgment at Nuremberg*; and the very strange *Touch of Evil*. We also had *An Evening With Marlene Dietrich*, a 54-minute TV special that would likely be the most popular of the bunch.

"I have a friend who does her," Mikey said. "He might be willing to make an appearance."

"We only have six tapes to rent. This is really all we need to do to keep them rented for the next three weeks."

"We could get more copies."

"It'll take a month for them to arrive. This is plenty."

Missy came out from behind the counter. She wore flannel and denim, and her hair flew everywhere. "So, like, who's Marlene Dietrich?" She pronounced her first name Mar-*Leen* and Mikey rolled his eyes.

"You really need to give people a test before you let them work here."

I liked Missy, though. She never told me what to do. And she hadn't known Jeffer. She'd begun working at Pinx after he died. We'd had one brief conversation about him, which ended with her saying, "That is so sad." And then she seemed to forget all about him before the end of that short sentence.

"Marlene Dietrich was a very famous German actress," I explained. "You should take one of her movies home."

"In a couple of weeks. When interest dies down," Mikey instructed.

"Someone should be behind the counter," I said, and then went back to my office and looked through the brochures the studios sent planning out next month's video order.

About a half an hour later, Mikey stuck his head into the office. "We have a situation."

"We do?"

"I wouldn't bother you, but it's Guy Peterson's boyfriend."

"Guy had a boyfriend?"

"Yes, didn't you know that?"

"No. I had no idea."

"Anyway, he rented five videos the day before the riots started and he's only bringing them back now. I told people they had to get the videos in by Tuesday in order to avoid late charges."

"Wait, that's not what I told you to do. I told you no late fees no matter when they brought the videos back."

"Yes, but that was ridiculously generous. I mean, his videos are six days late. That's sixty dollars in late fees. I think we can bring it down to twenty and he'll be—"

"What's his name?" I asked, pushing my way out of the office.

"Ted. Ted Bain."

"Thanks."

A few seconds later, I was walking up to a guy just a year or two younger than me. He had long hair cut in a chin-length bob. It was a terrible haircut, but it looked good on him—

mainly because any haircut would look good on him. He had wide cheeks and a square jaw; features that were strong and perfectly formed. I guessed that he'd take an amazing photograph. Which might explain how he met Guy the Camera Guy.

"Hi, Ted?"

"Yes?"

"I'm Noah Valentine. I'm the owner of Pinx."

"Look, this all a misunderstanding. I'll just pay the sixty dollars."

"I understand you were Guy Peterson's boyfriend?"

"Yeah, who are you again?"

"Noah. Anyway, you don't owe any late fees."

"Okay, well, thanks." He walked away. The videos were all on the counter. Three new releases and two pornos. I hurried to catch up with him.

We were out on the sidewalk by the time I said, "You should know that the police were in asking about Guy's friends."

"Here? They came here?"

"Yes."

"You talked to the police?"

"Yes, they came in and asked if I knew any of Guy's friends."

"Why did they come here? Why did they come talk to you?"

"Guy's family gave them my name. I met them when I went by to pick up a couple of videos Guy rented before the riots."

"You pick up videos? You mean I could have called and had those picked up a couple of days ago?"

"Well, no, we don't actually do that. It's just—I saw that Guy's shop had burned down. I figured he had a lot going on. So—I was being nice. I didn't know he was dead."

"So, you were hoping to see him?"

"To pick up the videos." He was looking at me like I was the biggest crook in Los Angeles. "It's lunch time. Can I buy you a taco? Or a pop?" I waved vaguely down the block at Taco Maria.

"Pop?"

"Soda. I grew up in the Midwest."

He looked at me for a moment and then said, "Maybe you'd better."

Taco Maria was in the same building, but they'd painted their storefront a very orange terra cotta—which might have been the reason the landlord would not let us paint our part pink. There were just six booths inside and murals on two of the walls, both depicting a crowd of primitive people swimming at a beach. There was no waitress. I went up to the order window and asked for two chicken taco combo plates and two medium Cokes.

I took the pop back to the table we'd claimed and sat down to wait for our lunches. Before I could decide what to ask Ted first, he said, "I know who you are. Guy told me he tried to have sex with you once and you freaked out."

"It wasn't that long after my lover died."

"That's weird. I heard death makes people horny."

I ignored that. "I have some of Guy's photos. Maybe you'd like to have them."

He just stared at me. I think I was confusing him somehow. I continued, "His sister put them in the alley, you know, throwing them away. I rescued them."

"Which photos do you have?"

"I only got two boxes. You can come and look at them if you'd like."

"No, thank you."

"Did Guy need money for some reason?"

"What do you mean?"

"I spoke to someone he knew. I don't want to say who, but Guy was trying to blackmail him. Over some photos he'd taken."

"How do you know all these things?"

"I really don't know much. You probably know more than I do. For instance, why Guy was trying to blackmail—" I almost said Rex but at the last minute finished my sentence with "... this person? Why did Guy need money?"

"That's none of your business."

"See, I went to the camera shop. After it burned—"

"Why would you do that?"

"I was curious."

"Stop. Stop being curious."

"No, you see, when I went to the camera store it didn't look like it had been looted—

"Stop."

He was visibly shaking. Very quietly he got up and walked out of the taco place. The food arrived while I was still trying to understand why he'd just gotten up and left.

"Um, could you put that in a box to go?" I asked the server/cook. "My friend changed his mind."

———

It was dark when I got back to my apartment, around nine o'clock. A single Tiki light burned over the table in the court-yard. Marc was stacking the last of the remnants from dinner. Presumably, Louis was inside doing dishes. It looked as though Leon had already left, if he'd been at all.

Marc saw me as he juggled dishes. "Well, hello stranger."

Stopping on the stairs to the second floor, I asked, "How was the opera?"

"Best four-hour nap I've ever had."

"Marc's not an opera buff." Louis came out and took the dishes from Marc.

"Louis' first partner was the conductor of the San Antonio Philharmonic. Louis learned music by osmosis. The kind of osmosis that can get you arrested in twenty-six states."

Louis ignored him and instead said, "So, No-ra, we heard you had an adventure."

"Yes, I met Rex Hoffman."

"How was that?"

Given that he'd just called me Nora, I figured he already new everything. "Not as much fun as Leon wanted it to be. It was interesting, though. I think Guy needed money for something."

"Maybe he was trying to burn the place down for insurance," Marc suggested.

"He didn't own the building."

"But the cameras must be insured. Maybe he was trying to burn the place down and accidentally got stuck inside."

"Did he accidentally stab himself with the spanner wrench?" Louis asked.

"We don't know that anyone got stabbed with that. And we only *think* there's blood on it. We haven't done any testing," Marc pointed out. Not that we had access to testing.

"Guys, I'm tired. Can we talk about this tomorrow?"

"Yes, of course," Louis said. "We're meeting for drinks tomorrow at New York, New York. About six."

Only in Los Angeles would someone name a bar New York, New York. It was in Atwater Village, which was a sliver of a neighborhood between Los Feliz and Glendale, bordering the 5 freeway. It wasn't a bad place to put a bar if you wanted an after-work crowd. It was easy to stop there if you were going home from Burbank, Glendale, Silver Lake, or even downtown. They sold two-for-one cocktails from five to eight, making it a great place to wait out rush hour traffic.

I hadn't been in a while, so I said, "All right, that sounds fun."

Finally, I continued up the stairs to my apartment. I could have told them about meeting Guy's boyfriend, but it had been a long day. I'd tell them tomorrow at New York, New York.

Inside my apartment, I threw my keys into a dish on the bookshelf by the door and hit the answering machine I kept on the small table next to the sofa. There was a message from my doctor asking to move my appointment from next Thursday to next Friday. That wasn't going to be a problem. There were two hang-ups and then a message from my mother. She said, "Call me when you get in. It doesn't matter what time. We need to talk."

When it came to my mother, "We need to talk" could mean just about anything. It could mean she was about to have surgery or it could mean she couldn't decide what kind of oil to put into her 1978 Dodge Aspen, both were given the same urgency.

It was one o'clock in the morning back in Michigan, so I was not going to call her. We could talk in the morning. Probably far too early in the morning for my taste.

I put in a CD, *Sunday in the Park with George*, a favorite, though why a musical whose theme was art and children appealed to me seemed odd since I had no interest in either. Pouring a glass of cheap chardonnay, I sat down at the dining table and looked out at the basin. It would have appealed to George Seurat, all the little points of light.

Why had Ted Bain run away from me? Why had he told me to stop being curious? Well, obviously there was something he didn't want me to know. Something that made him nervous. Had Ted killed Guy? That would explain why he wanted me to stop being curious, but it seemed wrong somehow. Killing your boyfriend was a crime of passion, spontaneous, the result of conflict. Why would Guy and Ted have such a conflict at the camera store? People were passionate at home or at backyard parties or bars—

My phone was ringing. I'd left the receiver on the table, so I was able to pick up without even moving. "Hello?"

"Isn't it a tragedy?" It was my mother.

"What is?"

"Marlene Dietrich. She's gone."

I got up and turned down the CD player. George was finishing the hat and now I'd barely be able to hear it.

"Mom, they said in the paper she was ninety."

"Time is such a cruel thing."

"I hope you live to be ninety."

"Thank you, dear, that's sweet. You'll be fifty-five when I'm ninety."

"Yes." Though why that was import—

"How old would Jeffer have been?"

"I don't know," I said. All I could really think about was the fact that he was thirty-eight when he died. And it was too confusing to add or subtract anything from that.

"She was such a good person."

"Who was?"

"Marlene Dietrich. You know she did so much during the war. She hated the Nazis. Hated what they did to her country."

"I made a shelf for her at the store. Most of the videos rented, so now it's kind of empty."

"Oh that's lovely. You know, you should open a video store here. I don't even know where I'd go to rent a Marlene Dietrich movie."

"Mom, you have cable. They'll be playing her movies all day long on American Movie Classics."

"It's not the same. A video store is like a library, you get to wander around and discover things."

"Why are you up so late?"

"Oh, I don't know. I worry. Are you seeing anyone, Noah? It's been almost two years."

"I'm fine. Thank you, though."

"For what?"

"For worrying about me."

7

New York, New York was located in a square little building that sat in the middle of a dusty parking lot. That Friday, the parking lot was full and it was hard to find a place to put the Sentra. Finally, I found what might have been the last spot. I was running late. It was almost seven. Denny had screwed up a charge and each time he tried to fix it, it added another charge instead. I'd ended up chatting with VISA for about twenty minutes trying to get it all reversed.

New York, New York was a relatively simple place. The bar with its line of green vinyl stools was on the left as you came in. There was a large, open space where there were bar-height tables and stools. In the back were restrooms and a storage room, and maybe an office. The big feature, though, was a black iron silhouette of the New York City skyline, which was attached to the long wall across from the bar.

It was packed when I walked in. George Michael was singing "Father Figure" over the stereo system. Most of the crowd wore business suits. In front of me was a sea of gray and blue wool, crisply laundered cotton shirts and loosened silk ties in a rainbow of "power" colors. I looked out of place in a pair of stonewashed jeans and a black cashmere V-neck sweater. I squeezed my way to the bar and ordered a Stoli and tonic from the overflow bartender. I would have preferred a glass of chardonnay, but it would have left me feeling even more out of place. I waved down the bar at the other bartender, Red. Red worked most of the shift on his own. He only had help during happy hour.

I paid my three dollars plus a one buck tip, picked up the two Stoli and tonics the bartender made for me, and sloshed my way around the bar looking for Marc and Louis. I found them in the corner by the music, then set one of the drinks on top of the jukebox.

"So Guy's boyfriend came into Pinx yesterday," I yelled over the music and chatter.

"Really?"

"What's he like?"

"He looks like a model. There are probably pictures of him in one of the boxes."

"Was he devastated?" Marc asked.

"He was freaked out, but I wouldn't say devastated. He told me to stop."

"Stop what?"

"Being curious, I guess."

"There must be something he doesn't want you to know."

"That's what I think," I said. "But I have no idea what."

"Did he look like a killer?" Marc asked.

"What does a killer look like?" Louis wanted to know.

Marc rolled his eyes. "I know anyone can be a killer, but there's usually something. Every time I see a picture of a killer in the newspaper, I think, oh yeah, that makes total sense."

"He seemed too nervous to be a killer," I said. "He was actually shaking."

"Well, if he's not hiding that he killed Guy, he must be hiding that he knows who did," Marc suggested.

"But if he knows who killed Guy why isn't he telling the police?" Louis asked.

Behind me someone said, "What are *you* doing here?"

64

My drink soured in my stomach and I turned around to see my former friend, Robert. In his early-thirties, Robert was tall and pink with a fuzz of blond hair floating around his head. He worked as a costumer, which inevitably meant his fashion choices were doubtful. That evening he wore a six-foot long white, tasseled scarf wrapped over and over around his neck. He lived for Latin boys and if you weren't a Latin boy there were times he didn't even see you. In fact, I was surprised he was seeing me at all.

Next to him stood his best friend—and my onetime friend —Tina. Small, blonde and ethereal, she was dressed in a floral-patterned drop-waist dress with a white T-shirt underneath and demi boots. It was the uniform of D-girls, which she aspired to be.

"Nice to see you, too, Robert."

"Tina, look what the cat dragged in," he said.

"I saw. My cat drags in dead chipmunks. Somehow this is worse." She had a hurt look in her eyes when she said it, like it was terrible of me to make her be mean.

"This is my neighborhood, you know. If you want to avoid me you should stick to your side of town." They were both committed Westsiders, and wouldn't have been caught dead in Silver Lake unless someone—probably the *LA Weekly*—had convinced them it was *the* place to be.

"I'm so sorry if you got the idea we were trying to avoid you, Noah," Robert said, drolly. "Avoiding you implies we actually care one way or the other, and believe me we have absolutely no interest in you."

Just then Louis poked his head around me. "Aren't you going to introduce us to your friends, Noah?"

"Oh, they're not friends of mine. They're just people I once knew."

"Now I'm even more interested. I'm Louis and this is my partner Marc. We're Noah's neighbors. How do you know him?"

"We're friends of Jeffer," Tina said, with as much drama as she could muster.

"Oh yes, the dead boyfriend," Louis said. Then he turned to me and said, "You seem to know a lot of dead guys."

I opened my mouth to object, but I did a quick count— Guy, Jeffer, my father, one our first employees at Pinx, a couple of guys I waited tables with, this guy I dated for a month or so before—and I had to admit, I knew a lot of dead guys.

"Well," Robert said. "We need to go. It was unpleasant running into you."

"Where did you meet such awful people," Louis asked me, loud enough that people actually turned around to gape.

"We're not awful people," Tina said. "We're loyal people."

"If it's any of your business, Noah treated Jeffer horribly at the end," Robert said.

"That's not true," I said weakly.

"Whatever," he said. "I don't care anymore." Though obviously he did. Paula Abdul began singing "Rush, Rush" as they walked away. A few minutes later I saw them walking out of the bar. I wondered if my car would be keyed when I went out to go home.

"They were charming," Louis said.

"Yes, I want a set of my own," Marc said.

"Do you want to tell us why they hate you so much?"

"Not really," I said. Then Louis did something I was grateful for. He left me alone and changed the subject. "Oh, Marc found something in the newspaper."

"I did, that's right. I even cut it out so I could bring it, but then I left it at home."

"Is it Guy's obituary?"

"Better," Louis said. "They're having a memorial for Guy tomorrow at one. It's in North Hollywood, so the three of us will have to leave by noon."

"I don't know if that's such a good idea," I said. Ted's nervousness weighed on me.

"It's a great idea. You're going and not another word about it," said Marc. It was too loud to really argue, so I did the easy thing and agreed.

An hour later, the bar had nearly cleared. Marc and Louis

went to pick up a pizza, while I stayed to finish my drink. There was a spot at the bar, so I went and took a stool.

Red came down and asked if I wanted another drink. I declined but took the opportunity to ask, "You know everyone, Red, did you know Guy Peterson?"

"Guy the Camera Guy? Yeah, I guess. He'd come in every couple of weeks. He offered to take some classy nudes of me once. I said sure but managed to be busy every time he tried to set it up."

"You don't want photos like that for posterity?"

"Posterity can go screw itself. He was just trying to get into my pants."

"Did he do that a lot? Try to get guys to model?"

"I wouldn't say a lot. But fairly often. Every now and then some kid would get super excited thinking it was their big break."

"Do you think any of those kids might want to kill Guy?"

He shrugged. "People say they want to kill each other all the time. I never take them seriously. Why are you asking that? I thought Guy died in a fire?"

"He may have. He may not have."

"A man of mystery. Come on, let me buy you a drink."

I let him. I didn't mind cold pizza one bit.

I was having a dream about Jeffer; I had them a lot. In this one I was angry and screaming at him. I couldn't tell what I was screaming. Sound was coming out of my mouth but no words. A raging emotion coming out of my mouth and speeding toward Jeffer, making him cower. And then he pushed his way forward, his hand closing over my mouth, silencing me—

I woke up. It was very dark. Someone was sitting on top of me, straddling my chest, a hand over my mouth. I couldn't get enough air to scream or yell. I struggled a moment and he shushed me.

"If you promise not to yell I'll take my hand away." I recognized the voice. My eyes must have gotten very wide. It was Guy Peterson. Alive. And on top of me. "Do you promise?"

I nodded my head. He removed his hand, I gasped for breath. As soon as I was able, I hissed, "You're not dead."

"No, I'm not."

"Who is dead? Who did they find in your store?"

"It's not safe to tell you that."

"Did you kill him?"

"It's not safe to tell you that either." My guess was he did kill whomever it was they found in his store. If he hadn't it would be safe to tell me. The question was, did he kill the man in self-defense?

"Did you have to kill him?"

"Stop asking questions. Stop poking around."

"Why won't you—Ted Bain has been hiding you, hasn't he?"

"You need to mind your own business."

"He can't hide you forever. Eventually the police will figure out he's your boyfriend."

"Yeah, well, don't be the one to tell them. In fact, don't even talk to them."

"I can't—" I stopped. What would Guy do if I told him I'd call the police the minute he left? Was he threatening me? That didn't seem likely. "Why shouldn't I talk to the police?"

"Because they'll kill you."

It was a shocking thing to say. Not just because of what it meant, but because of the way he said it. With such certainty. He was sure they'd kill me.

"You can't tell anyone you saw me. Everyone who knows I'm alive is in danger."

"Well, thanks for stopping by, then."

"You were already in danger. You're asking too many questions. Don't ask any more."

Then he got off me, and walked out of my apartment. I waited a moment. My heart was pounding and I had a little trouble catching my breath. Calmer, I walked out into the living room. One of my windows was wide open and the screen was off. That was how Guy had gotten in. I went to the corner windows over my desk and looked down. I could see down to the street. A little red sports car was illegally parked in front of the garage. I couldn't see who was in the car, but I didn't need to.

Ted Bain.

8

I COULDN'T SLEEP. BIG SURPRISE. I PULLED THE TWO BOXES of photos out of my bedroom closet and brought them out to the living room. I dumped them all on the dining table. I divided the photos into stacks and separated them into three simple categories: safe, semi-dangerous and dangerous. In the safe pile went all of the landscapes and cityscapes taken at a distance—it was hard to blackmail a tree or a building. In the semi-dangerous pile I put anything with a person in it, just in case. Most of the "artistic" nudes went into that pile, figuring they weren't graphic enough to blackmail anyone over. The dangerous pile was the smallest. In it, I put all of the artsy photos of the Rodney King-like beating and a couple of other explicitly sexual photos which, depending on who they were of, could be used for blackmail.

Of course, there was the box I didn't have. The box that Guy's sister was about to dump into the garbage. Seeing that I'd taken the others, she might have kept it. Or, she might not have. And for all I know, every single photo in there could be used to blackmail someone.

I went back to the artsy photos of the white guy being beaten. Guy had told me to be afraid of the police. Well, no, he'd said they'd kill me if I knew too much. Did these photos constitute knowing too much? I spread them out and studied them. I looked at all the faces. I didn't recognize anyone. There seemed to be floodlights behind the camera giving the photos a very 'shocking' look. All they needed to be a fashion shoot was a couple of models in satin dresses wandering around amid the violence.

I finally fell asleep at the table while, studying the photos, at about four in the morning. Six hours later, I woke up with an eight by ten stuck to my face and someone knocking on my door.

Opening the door, I found Marc and Louis standing there in well-tailored dark suits. Louis raised his eyebrows when he saw me—gym shorts, wife-beater, a terminal case of bedhead.

"You're not ready."

"Oh, gosh, maybe you guys should go without me."

"Don't be silly. No one's going to slap our wrists if we're a little tardy," Marc said.

"Get in the shower. I'll make coffee," Louis added as they pushed by me into the apartment.

Reluctantly, I went to get ready. Fifteen minutes later, I was showered and shaved. I pushed my hair around until it almost looked styled.

Standing in front of my closet in a towel, I studied my meager choices. The only suit I had was the one I wore to Jeffer's funeral. I'd sworn I would never wear it again. A promise that might have been easier to keep if I'd given it away to charity. My other options were limited. I could go with a pair of black jeans and a black T-shirt, but that was more appropriate for joining a motorcycle gang than attending a funeral.

I had two jackets, one was black with a windowpane pinstripe and the other was chartreuse. Both were from the late eighties and had gigantic shoulder pads. Chartreuse was wrong for a funeral. In fact it was wrong for most things. When I bought it Jeffer asked if I had dreams of becoming a pimp. I did not. I think I wore the jacket once.

Louis stuck his head into the bedroom. "Knock, knock, I hope you're decent." He set a cup of coffee onto the built-in dresser that took up most of the wall behind the door. "There was some Kahlúa in your cupboard, so I spiked your coffee."

He retreated, closing the door behind him. I went and retrieved the coffee. There was no other option. I was going to have to wear the black-and-white jacket with the shoulder pads. I put on the black jeans, a white oxford shirt, a silver tie and the offending jacket. It was best I could do. My shirt needed ironing and my shoes were scuffed, but I was ready.

I drank the rest of my coffee, as I stepped out into the living room.

"What are you doing with the photos?" Marc asked.

"I couldn't sleep, so I looked through them."

"See anything interesting?"

"Not really."

I couldn't mention that the meaning of the photos was now very different. There was some danger there I wasn't seeing. A danger I didn't want to include them in.

"I'm ready," I said.

Marc looked at me quizzically. "Aren't you going to do your hair?"

"Oh, God."

After I spent another five minutes prodding and coaxing and pasting my hair so that it looked deliberate, we left. Louis drove a two-year-old beige Honda something or other with velour seats and a sunroof. We could have taken Marc's Infiniti, but they didn't want to add unnecessary miles to the lease. I sat in the backseat and watched the city go by for a few minutes. When he pulled onto the 101 going north, I asked, "Where is the memorial?"

"It's at a funeral home in North Hollywood."

"North Hollywood? Why?"

"I imagine they had trouble getting it. It's kind of a busy weekend for funerals."

I hadn't thought about that. The death total for the riots was now over sixty. And of course that didn't include the stress-related heart attacks. Those weren't counted and published in the newspaper. Funerals had to be happening all over the city at a breakneck pace.

"Louis, tell him the name of the place we're going," Marc said.

"International Funeral Home of Pancakes," he said, cackling.

"It is not," I said.

"No, but it's close. It's something like International Funeral Homes of America." That was nearly as bad. How something could be international and national at the same time was beyond me.

We were heading through the Cahuenga Pass, when Louis asked, "Noah? Do you think they cremated him?"

"Oh, Louis," Marc said.

"All right, this is stopping before we get there. You cannot crack jokes at this thing," I said.

"Not even if I whisper?"

"Even if you whisper."

When we got to North Hollywood, the funeral home was something of a shock. It was a single story building with no windows, a double Mediterranean front door and a "decorative" wall made out of concrete blocks. The parking lot around the building was cracked, with weeds growing through the cracks.

After he finished parking, Louis looked over the front seat and said, "The VFW hall must have been booked."

"Louis," Marc and I said at the same time.

We got out of the car and made our way into the funeral home. There were three separate rooms: Serenity, Eternity and Tranquility. The Peterson Memorial was in the Tranquility room at the back of the building.

As we entered, there was a large photo on an easel. It was Guy Peterson's high school graduation photo. He looked awkward and a little feral. His features hadn't yet morphed into the attractive man he'd become. The high school picture seemed an odd choice for the Petersons to make. Perhaps they wanted to use a photo from a time when he was completely theirs. But still, it made it seem we were attending a memorial service for a teenager. A tragedy much worse than this one.

Though I didn't know who we were really memorializing, I didn't think it was a teenager. Given Guy's fear of the police, I'd say the dead guy was a policeman. I tried to remember if I'd seen anything about a missing policeman after the riots; I knew there were missing people, well over a hundred. Was one of them a policeman? Or some kind of informant? And what was Guy's real connection to the police?

The room was half-full. On one side of the room there was a collection of familiar looking guys, neighborhood guys who might have been Guy's friends (or tricks) and also rented videos from me. On the other side of the room were Guy's parents standing with a young woman in an off-the-shoulder black minidress. I wouldn't have recognized her except for the way she glared at the obviously gay men on the other side of the room. It was his sister, Cindy.

She cleaned up better than expected, though when I looked close I noticed the toughness I'd seen earlier. She was a little too tall—and her three-inch heels just made things worse—and too wide to wear that dress. She looked like the kind of woman who carried a shiv in her purse, next to the blood red lipstick.

"There's no coffin," Marc said.

"I told you—"

"Shut up."

"It's a memorial," I said. "Memorials happen without the body."

"So where is his body?"

Just then Javier O'Shea walked in. I said, "I don't know, let me try to find out." And I walked to the back of the room.

"I thought you barely knew Guy Peterson?" O'Shea said when I got over to him. His eyes were a dusty brown, about the same tone as his skin. In combination with his ink-black hair they were far too distracting.

"Guy was an acquaintance. Is there some Miss Manners rule I missed about attending a memorial for an acquaintance?"

"It's just odd, that's all."

I studied him for a moment then said, "Wait, I've seen this in a movie. The police go to funerals because they think the killer will, too."

"And usually the killer walks up to the policeman and says something almost exactly like that."

"I can guarantee you, I didn't kill Guy Peterson." I said, with absolute confidence.

"I don't think you did."

"So, there's no coffin," I mentioned, the point of my walking over.

"We haven't released the body. When we do we'll send it to Fresno and the Petersons will have a graveside service."

"May I ask why you haven't released the body?" I asked, though I knew it might have something to do with Guy's being in my bedroom just a few hours before.

"No you may not, but I'll tell you anyway. We're waiting on dental records. In case you haven't heard, there were over sixty deaths in the last week and a half. We're not prepared for that kind of caseload."

"I have to say, I'm surprised the Petersons are doing this. They're not exactly friendly."

"We asked them to. We're still interested in talking to as many of Guy's friends as we can."

I glanced around the room again. I couldn't tell you whether these were Guy's friends or not. They could easily be gawkers.

"If you want to talk to Guy's friends, you'd do better to go to Detour tonight around ten o'clock."

"Are you telling me he was a whore?"

"You don't have to be a whore to go to Detour."

"No. But you do if you want everyone in Detour to know your name."

Something about his saying that set off my gaydar like a five-alarm fire. A straight policeman would assume all gay guys were whores. Javier O'Shea didn't do that.

"Where's your partner?" I asked.

"Busy. The partner thing is kind of casual. On an 'as needed' basis."

"I see. It took two of you to talk to me the other day, but one of you can handle an entire memorial service?"

"There are a lot of factors involved, geography, caseload. But you're not really interested in my job, are you?"

No. I wasn't. I was interested in knowing if he was as dangerous as Guy said. And I was interested in knowing why he was dangerous. Other than that I didn't really care too much about his job.

"If you'll excuse me, I should get back to my friends."

"Did they know Guy Peterson?"

"Never met him," I lied.

He nodded and I walked away. Right after I got back to Marc and Louis, Pachelbel's Canon in D got pumped in over the speakers. That seemed to be a cue for everyone to sit down.

As the music was playing, Louis leaned over and asked, "Who was that you were talking to?"

"Policeman. They haven't released the body yet." And wouldn't since Guy wasn't dead, but it wasn't safe to say that. "They're waiting on dental records."

"They're not even sure Guy Peterson is dead?" Louis asked. Marc shushed us.

A minister from some sort of generic Christianity appeared in front of us and began the memorial. There wasn't much to it, fortunately. The minister spoke about Guy for a few minutes, though it was obvious they'd never met. Then each of his family members got up and said a few words. His mother told a story about what a clever toddler he was. His father talked about his days as a Frontier Scout. His sister about her big brother standing up for her when she was bullied in school—though, I found it hard to believe she'd ever been bullied. I wondered if they were reading from scripts, and not just because their stories didn't fit with the man I'd met. Their stories barely fit with who they seemed to be.

When it was over, we all stood and awkwardly began shuffling out of the stuffy room.

"Your policeman is sexy," Louis said.

"He's not my policeman."

"Maybe he should be," Marc said.

Great, I thought, *they're trying to fix me up with the most dangerous person in the room.*

9

"SO I'M FRIENDLY WITH A WOMAN NAMED PEARL, WHO'S the assistant to our in-house counsel. She has LexisNexis on her desktop," Louis said. He worked at a private hospital that focused on the most profitable procedures, plastic surgery and in vitro fertilization. He had something to do with their proprietary software programs but didn't talk much about his work. It wasn't a glamorous job. Unlike Marc and Leon, whose jobs were assumed to be more glamorous than they probably were.

"Okay? What is LexisNexis?" I had no idea where Louis was going with this, but it barely mattered since I had an enormous margarita in front of me. We'd left the memorial around one thirty, taken almost an hour to drive back to Silver Lake since there was an accident on the 170, and it was now well past lunchtime. Louis had driven directly to La Casita Grande without asking. We didn't complain.

"LexisNexis is like Prodigy or America Online but for lawyers. A legal research service. You have to use a modem to dial into it. Very expensive."

"I see," I said, though I didn't. I had no idea what he was talking about. Half the things he'd just mentioned I'd never heard of.

"Anyway, she did a search on the camera store's address and we came up with the landlord's name: Sherman Dooley."

"Right, that's his name," I said, slipping out of my awful jacket with its gigantic shoulders and undoing my tie.

"Well, Mr. Dooley has had three other buildings burn."

"Really?"

"His insurance company is going to have a field day with that," Marc said.

"He'll be lucky if he gets paid," Louis agreed.

But, Dooley didn't burn the building down. I knew that. Or did I? Guy was alive. Someone else was dead. I assumed he'd killed that person and set the fire, but did I know that? Actually, I didn't.

"Dooley is like seventy years old. I don't think he killed whoever it was in the building."

"Whoever it was the building?" Louis repeated. "You mean, Guy Peterson. Whose memorial we just went to."

"Yes, I mean Guy Peterson," I said, my face flushing. "This is what happens when you wake me up with Kahlúa."

They both looked at me suspiciously. I took a moment to look around. I'd always liked La Casita Grande. It was built in an old mansion and had a half a dozen rooms on the first floor. The room we were in was painted red with what looked like Mexican artifacts on the wall but were probably things you could buy at a swap meet across the border in Tijuana.

"Where's Leon?" I asked, to distract them. "I would have thought he'd love a good memorial."

"He says he gave them up for Lent."

"Lent is over."

"Not for Leon. Every Lent he gives up something he hates and then does it year-round."

"That doesn't sound very Catholic," I said.

"I think it's a great idea," Marc said. "Next year I'll give up work for Lent and then never go back."

"No dear, you're not doing that."

The waiter stopped by and we ordered another round of margaritas, an order of guacamole and a couple of quesadillas.

When he was gone, Louis turned to me and said, "So, Noah, I swear I heard some funky noises coming from your bedroom last night. I thought you might be getting lucky; now I'm not so sure."

"I slept like a baby," I lied.

"Yeah, most babies don't sleep through the night," Louis pointed out. "You certainly didn't."

They were staring at me. On the one hand, if they knew Guy was alive I'd be putting them in danger; on the other if I had another margarita I'd tell them so I might as well do it now.

"Guy Peterson is alive."

"I knew it," Louis practically yelled.

"You did not," Marc said doubtfully.

"All right, I almost knew it," Louis admitted. "So he came to your apartment last night?"

"He crawled in through the window while I was asleep."

"I would have screamed," Marc said.

"I woke up with his hand over my mouth, so I couldn't."

"Oh my God, that sounds awful."

"It wasn't fun."

"So, what do you think that means?" asked Louis.

"Well, it means someone else burned to death in that building," I said.

"Did Guy mention the identity of…oh, let's call him Mr. Crispy?"

"Louis, don't call him that. For all we know he was a nice guy."

"For all we know he was not."

"Guy said it was too dangerous to tell me who Mr. C—who was in the building. And speaking of dangerous, he said anyone who knows he's alive is in danger. I may have just put your lives at risk."

They looked at each other and broke out laughing. The waiter arrived with our new margaritas.

"Wait, did Guy kill whoever it was they found in the camera store? No, see that's too long, we have to call him Mr. Crispy."

Marc just rolled his eyes.

"My guess is yes. Guy killed Mr. Crispy," I admitted.

"Oooh, sex with a murderer," Marc said. "That's kind of exciting."

"I did not have sex with Guy. He showed up. Told me to stop poking around. And left."

"Are you going to? Stop poking around?" Louis asked.

"Yes, of course, I don't want to end up dead."

"You're off to a bad start, you know. Coming to the memorial with us."

"I wouldn't have gone if you hadn't dragged me."

"Oh we did not drag you," Marc said. "You said 'maybe we should go without you' and we said 'no' and that was it. That's not dragging you."

"And you didn't have to flirt with that policeman. Which I'm pretty sure would come under the definition of 'poking around.'"

Oh my God, I thought, *they're right*. I *was* still poking around. Which was dangerous. "Well," I said. "I'm going to stop poking around. As of now."

"Mmmm-hmmm. Good luck with that." Marc sipped his drink.

"This may sound like a stupid question, but did you tell Detective Sexy Cop that Guy Peterson is alive?" Louis asked.

"Oh my God, no."

"Why not? It seems like the kind of thing you should tell the police."

"That's the danger part. The LAPD. He said they'd kill anyone who knows he's alive."

They looked at each other and frowned. Now it didn't seem as funny. The waiter came and we ordered far too much food. Once he left, Louis said, "Let's recap. What do we know for sure?"

"Guy Peterson is alive," I said.

"We have a mystery corpse," Marc added.

"Mr. Crispy."

"Louis."

"The police are dangerous," he said, ignoring Marc.

"No, Louis, we don't know that," Marc corrected. "We know Guy *says* the police are dangerous. He could just be saying that to keep Noah away from them."

"We know that Guy tried to blackmail Rex Hoffman," I said.

"No, again, we only know that Rex *said* that. Rex could have lied."

"But we know that the photos of Rex exist and that Rex is aware of them. I'd say it's *likely* Guy tried to blackmail Rex."

"I'd agree with that," Marc said. "The thing we can't be sure of is whether he succeeded."

"Why would Rex lie about that?" I asked.

"You could have tried blackmailing him, too. Saying he didn't pay made that a lot harder."

"There are also those 'artsy' photographs of the Frontier Scouts beating that white guy," Louis said.

"But that's art," I said. "You don't threaten people over art."

"Why not?" he asked. "They're certainly provocative enough. I've been wondering if they might have something to do with the Trailblazers."

"The whats?" I asked.

"Trailblazers. It's a program the Frontier Scouts have with the LAPD. They're supposed to learn about law enforcement, but mainly they just answer the phone."

"You mean, when you call the police station you get a Frontier Scout? That doesn't seem right."

"That's what happened last year, when Marc's car was stolen. We called the police and reported it to a child whose voice hadn't even broken."

"Why anyone would steal a seven-year-old Honda Civic is beyond me," Marc said.

"That's why we got a brand new Infiniti. If someone steals it we'll at least know why."

"Okay, I see the connection to the Frontier Scouts in the picture, but I still don't understand it. Do you?"

"No," said Marc. "I still think it's a commentary on the

Rodney King beating, but…is he saying he didn't think it was about race? I mean, they're beating a white guy."

"They don't *just* beat black people," Louis said. "They used to come out and raid the gay bars, arrest people, beat up people."

"Actually, they raided a bar in Florida last year."

"This isn't Florida, Marc."

"If the best we can say for ourselves is that we're not Florida, we're not doing too well," I pointed out.

"You know, I think I know how we might get more information," Louis said. "Remember you asked about the uniforms, Noah? We'll go to the Gauntlet later."

"Oh, yes," said Marc. "Someone there will be in uniform. Maybe even one of the 'policemen' from the photos."

"No," I said as firmly as I could. "Guy told me to keep out of this and I think that's what we should do."

"Because we're in danger?" Louis asked.

"Well, yes…"

"Look, we know that Guy Peterson is alive. That means if we don't tell the police we're accessories after the fact or obstructing justice or breaking some other law."

"But if Guy's telling Noah the truth, going to the police is the worst thing we can do," Marc said.

"So we should do nothing," I said.

"No, we should figure out who's really dangerous. The police. Or Guy Peterson," Louis said.

Unfortunately, that made a lot of sense.

We stayed at Casita del Grande for another hour, then we went home and got ready to go to the Gauntlet. I was thrilled to get out of my funeral outfit. In fact, I hated it so much that I just threw it at the bottom of my closet, promising myself that if anyone else died I'd buy an actual, brand new black suit. I also promised myself I'd throw away the suit from Jeffer's funeral, since I was never going to wear it again, it was pointless to hold onto it.

I took a long shower ending with a blast of cold water. Dried my hair, then pushed it around until it looked a little like a brown volcano on the verge of erupting. I put on the pair of black Levis, again, and an extra small black T-shirt—I looked like the motorcycle club wannabe I hadn't wanted to look like at Guy's memorial. It was, however, appropriate for the Gauntlet.

Not that I had a lot of experience with places like the Gauntlet, since I didn't feel like I fit there. I hadn't actually found any place where I felt like I belonged. I felt too old to be a twink, too vanilla to be leather, too thin to be a bear. I wasn't fashionable or chic like the guys in West Hollywood, nor as offbeat and alternative as the guys in Silver Lake. I was sort of a nothing. A generic gay guy, if such a thing even existed.

Going down the stairs to meet Marc and Louis, I was very conscious of my black demi boots. They were wrong for the evening—though better than going barefoot. What I needed was motorcycle boots, but I didn't have those. The black half-boots with their pointed toe and two-inch heel were the best I could do.

Marc and Louis were a little better at this. Louis wore jeans, a white T-shirt and a black leather vest. And...he had motorcycle boots. Marc wore jeans, a blue mechanics shirt with the name Spud embroidered over his left pocket, and a leather motorcycle cap. They would both fit in so much better than I. But then couples always seemed to. Well, most couples.

After a brief discussion, we decided to take two cars. We should have taken one cab, but after four margaritas none of us were thinking that responsibly or even practically. The Gauntlet was only a few very steep blocks away, but by the time we'd found two parking places the gain was negligible.

Squeezed between an auto body repair shop and an awkward brick building that had at various times housed a real-estate office, an acupuncturist and a psychic, The Gauntlet was nondescript, like many gay bars. A black box of a building with the bar's name painted on it in letters you could barely see from the street. I found a place to park only a block away, so I was waiting in front of the bar when Marc and Louis got there.

"We're over on Manzanita. I can't imagine where we'd be if we'd waited until things got crowded," Marc said.

Inside, the Gauntlet it was already crowded. The Bronski Beat was singing "Small Town Boy," to which a bored young man in a leather jock strap was dancing. There was a circular bar with too many taps, a wall of lockers, and a couple of TV screens playing porn. Porn they rented from me at a special weekly rate.

Louis went to the bar to get us drinks, while Marc and I observed people. An older man with nipples the size of a pink eraser and his junk shoved into a saggy leather thong walked by. Marc leaned over and said into my ear, "I almost wore that outfit."

"Groove is in the Heart" by Deee-Lite began to play, bouncy, catchy dance music. Nobody danced. Except the kid on the stage and it was hard to tell if this was really the song he was dancing to.

Louis came back with a margarita on the rocks for Marc and two drafts. The drinks came in hazy plastic glasses. Louis was giving Marc a dirty look; blended drinks were always a no-no in a leather bar.

"What? Never mix never worry."

We sipped our drinks and looked around. I didn't see a lot of uniforms and wondered if they had their own special night. Louis tipped his head and we followed him into a smaller, darker room that had a row of raised seats where you could get your shoes shined by a submissive boot black. A gentleman in a policeman's uniform was having his boots worked over by a nearly naked guy putting in a lot of effort.

"Give me the picture," Louis said to me.

Before I walked out of my apartment I'd grabbed one of Guy's "artistic" beating photos, folded it and slid it into my back pocket. I handed it to Louis, who took it over to the fake-LAPD officer. They had a brief conversation and then Louis came back over to us.

"He knows half the guys in the picture."

"Did he know anything else about it?"

"He heard some things about the shoot," Louis said. "The kid who's getting beat-up, he's totally into it. You can't see it in the picture, but he was hard the whole time."

"Okay, interesting as that is, it doesn't really help," I said. "Why did Guy take pictures like this?"

"He doesn't know. He did say that Guy had everything written out exactly the way he wanted it."

"That's not surprising," I said.

"Apparently he had some trouble reading the notes, though."

"He couldn't read his own handwriting?"

"I've had it happen," Louis shrugged.

"Yeah, but this was a shoot that he'd arranged. It was important to him. If he wrote out what he wanted, well, wouldn't he remember even if he couldn't read his own handwriting?"

"Maybe Guy Peterson will show up in your bedroom again and you can ask him."

"I'd just as soon he *not* break into my apartment in the middle of the night."

"Should we try to talk to someone who was actually at the shoot?" Marc asked.

"He said one of the guys in the photo might be in later, but I'm not sure he'll know too much more."

"So does this answer the original question?" I asked.

"Which question is that?" Louis wanted to know.

"Oh my God, it's been like four hours and you don't remember," I said. "All we're trying to find out is whether it's Guy who's dangerous or whether it's the police."

"Ah, that question."

Louis and Marc both shrugged.

10

DETOUR WAS ON SUNSET BOULEVARD, A SMALL BUILDING with a large parking lot between it and the street. The front door was hung with several long strips of thick black rubber. I don't know if that was to keep bugs out or if it was a strange kind of sobriety test. Seriously, you had to be sober enough to get through it and if you weren't you didn't get in.

I almost didn't make it.

Inside, a large rectangular bar sat in the center of the room ringed by stools. I wobbled my way to the bar telling myself I was just there to walk through and then I'd go home. There was just one thing I—

The bartender asked me if I wanted something to drink so I ordered a Miller Lite and a shot of Cuervo. When he set the order in front of me, I handed him a ten and downed the shot.

"I was going to ask if you wanted salt and a lemon with that," he said.

"I guess not," I said, as I picked up the beer and walked away. I think I left him a really good tip. The crowd at Detour was different than the Gauntlet but not by much. There were some guys in leather, guys who would end up at the Gauntlet or Cuffs later on. But then there were a lot of guys in Levis and T-shirts. T-shirts with logos for favorite bands or sports teams or political statements. There were at least two guys wearing Silence = Death T-shirts. I hoped they talked to each other; it would be ironic if they didn't.

Then I saw the person I was looking for, Detective Javier O'Shea. He looked completely out of place. There was no way he was gay, I was sure of it now. Yeah, there were always gay guys who were a little out of step—I was probably one of them—but he wore a yellow alligator shirt, jeans and a pair of top-siders; perfect for a cocktail cruise out of Marina del Rey but completely wrong for a Levi/leather bar in Silver Lake. I walked over and said, "Hello. What's a nice boy like you doing in a place like this?"

He backed up and waved a hand in front of his face. "Wow, I know what you've been doing since this afternoon."

"Oh, well excuse me. I'm in a bar smelling of alcohol. Heavens."

"Yeah, well, no one else in here will notice. Did you drive here?"

I held my finger up in front of my lips and shushed him. "Don't tell anyone. It's okay though, it's only a few blocks and I drive really slow."

"I've heard that one before."

"You don't drink?"

"Not on duty."

Drunk as I was, that didn't compute. If he was a dangerous cop like Guy said he was then why was he following the rules? Dangerous cops didn't follow rules. That's part of what makes them dangerous.

"Are you going to arrest me?" I asked.

"I'm not on patrol anymore. I don't arrest drunk drivers. I do think you should take a cab home."

"Whatever."

"So, do you know which of these men were friendly with Guy Peterson?"

"Oh my God, no. I almost never come here."

"Why did you come tonight?"

He had me there. I wasn't going to say 'To figure out if

you're really dangerous,' so I said, "I've had a few drinks and it was on the way home."

"So who could tell me who Guy Peterson's friends are?"

"Maybe the bartender," I said.

"Okay, thanks."

He started to walk over to the bar, but I grabbed his arm. "Hey wait a minute. I have two questions. Number one, why didn't you just get Guy's address book from his apartment?"

"There wasn't one there. We think it might have burned in the fire at the camera store."

"Oh, that sucks."

"And…"

"And it sucks a lot?"

"You had a second question."

"Oh, that's right. Why does it matter? Why do you have to talk to Guy's friends? It was the riots, right? I mean, that's why the store got burned down. So, why do his friends matter?"

"I can't discuss an active investigation with you."

"Okay, but what are you going to ask his friends?"

He looked at me sharply. "You knew Guy better than you're letting on, didn't you?"

"Okay, you can go talk to the bartender."

"Listen, I don't think you've done anything wrong. I just don't think you're telling me everything you know."

There was an understatement.

"Do you have any idea why Guy went to the camera store that afternoon?"

"No."

"Have you heard any rumors?"

"No."

"Do you know anyone who might want to kill Guy?"

Since the truth was, "You," I didn't say anything right off. Then I thought about what he was asking me. "You don't think this has anything to do with the riots, do you?"

Answering would be discussing an active investigation and I could see him trying not to do it.

"What do you think?" he asked.

"If you thought this was related to the riot you wouldn't be in here on a Saturday night."

I wondered if it might be safe to tell him that Guy was alive. Four words and the whole thing would be over. They were on the tip of my tongue when he said, "I've heard that you have two boxes of Peterson's photos. I'm going to need you to give those to me."

My mouth was dry. He wanted the photos. That meant he was probably as dangerous as Guy said.

"Why? His family was just throwing them out."

"Yes, I know. They shouldn't have done that. Everything was so chaotic after the riot. Procedure fell apart. We should have searched his apartment long before we did." He seemed disinterested, casual, and the conversation was anything but.

"Well, if you're working I'll leave you to it," I said, trying to meet his casualness.

"You don't have to run away," he said.

"I'm not. Your investigation is much more serious than I thought. I shouldn't get in the way of it." Or, become the target.

"How do you know?" he asked.

"How do I know your investigation is serious?"

"No, how do you know who likes you and how do they know you like them?"

"I don't think it's much different than how you pick-up a woman."

"It looks different. It looks a lot different."

I shrugged. "It's about the eyes. You look at a guy you like, and keep looking until he sees you looking. Then you look away for a second, and then look back to see if he's still looking at you. You do that for a bit until one of you smiles. Then you go over and start talking."

"What do you say?"

"Stupid stuff. You talk about the bar and how you don't come here very often, even if you come every night. You pay each other compliments; those don't have to be truthful either. If all you want is sex you ask if they live nearby pretty quickly."

"Do you talk about…"

"The kind of sex you want? Sometimes. But that can get dicey. There are guys who mostly just want to talk about sex. And then there are other guys who want you to be something specific but asking you to be that ruins it for them, so you're kind of guessing."

"That is different than with a girl."

"Is it really?"

"You never…with a woman?"

"I'm a gold star faggot."

He looked uncomfortable when I said that but went on anyway. "With a woman, yeah, there's the eye thing, but it goes on and on. Sometimes when a woman's interested in you she'll refuse to look in your direction, but at the same time she'll flip her hair or tip her head like she's having a photo taken. You can tell she knows you're looking at her. And then when you talk to her, even if all she wants is a one-night stand, she's got to act like it's a date, like she's interested in more. You pay her compliments, that's the same. But if you talk about sex too soon or sometimes even at all, that's it, you're blown out of the water."

I didn't quite understand the look on his face or why the conversation had taken this turn. I was desperate to get away from him but not ready to go home.

"So, do you live nearby?" he asked.

That sent a jolt up and down my spine. Was he asking? No, he couldn't be. It was a joke. Wasn't it?

"Good night, Detective. I'm going home now," I said and walked away.

Why had he asked if I lived nearby? He would already know where I lived. I mean, after questioning me at the video store wouldn't he at least have found out that much? For the file, at least?

Was he serious? Or was he just teasing?

I drove down to Pinx and parked in the lot behind the store. Then I walked a few blocks south to Cuffs and got in line outside the bar. I was number five, meaning I'd have to wait for four people to leave before they let me in. I slumped against the building and asked myself why I didn't just go home. Going home would be the smart thing to do. I was drunk and there wasn't anything inside that was going to change my life. Or at least not change my life in a positive way. Cars were going by. It was well after midnight. *Where were they going? Why were so many people still awake? Who was—*

A gray Crown Vic passed by on the opposite side of the street. For the briefest moment, I was sure I saw Detective Nino Percy in the driver's seat. I saw a flash of his face and then he was gone. *Had I really seen him?* I wondered. *Or was I just that drunk?*

I'd never been to Cuffs before. The first thing that people told you about the bar was that things happened there in the corners. Nasty, dirty things that were worth showing up in the middle of the night for. What they didn't tell you was how tiny the place was. It was really just one not very big room with a square bar in the middle. Oh, and wall to wall people. Very few of whom were actually sexy.

By the time I got inside, I'd realized something very important about gay bars in Silver Lake. They all had bars in the center of the room, unlike New York, New York, which had a bar on one side. At first I thought that was coincidental, but then—as I jumped into the stream of men walking one way round and round the bar looking at a different stream of men walking around the other way—it hit me: cruising. A bar in the middle of the room promoted cruising. A bar on one side discouraged it, because it was full of awkward turnarounds.

In front of me, an older gentleman in full leather smiled at whoever was behind me and said, "Hello, counselor."

Behind me a voice said, "Lovely evening, your honor."

I wanted to spin around and get a look at whatever he was wearing, but that seemed a bit obvious. And that was something I knew not to be at Cuffs. Obvious.

Men were reaching out and squeezing my shoulders, touching my chest. I began looking for a place to stand still—

and unaccosted. People leaned up against the postage stamp bar in the center of the room, but there didn't seem to be any room. Some other people were just standing around on the far side of the bar. I made for them.

The music was harsh, sharp-edged techno; really not much more than a drum, a snare and some random notes flitting around the steady beat. Eventually, I squeezed myself into a nonmoving corner where some guys were talking like they already knew one another. I watched the cruisers walk by and thought about struggling through the crowd to buy a Calistoga, but it seemed like too much trouble.

A guy passed by, catching my eye. He was over six foot, in his early forties, had curly hair with a few flecks of gray, and mustache straight out of seventies porn. There was something about him I liked, or maybe there was something about me he liked. I wasn't too sure which it was.

I watched as he made his way around the bar, picking him out as he weaved in and out of the mob. When I really looked around, I decided that the line outside was more to do with marketing than the fire code. There already were clearly too many people in the bar for the fire code. Making people wait to get in was just about getting more people to want to get in.

And then the tall guy was standing in front of me. Just standing. Looking down at me. Waiting for me to say something. Finally, I asked, "Do you have a name?"

"Of course I have a name, but does it matter?"

"Do you live around here?"

"No," he said, as he leaned in to kiss me.

The last man I kissed was Guy Peterson and that seemed like ancient history. This guy was aggressive, his tongue exploring my mouth, his hands wandering over my body. Before I knew it they were in my jeans. Unzipping them. Then—

This was what Cuffs was about. Little bits of sex shoved into the corners. No one could really see what you were doing. It was too dark and too crowded. It was a place so public it was private.

—I shoved away from him, zipped my jeans and roughly

pushed my way out of the bar. Once out in the street, I was breathing heavily, shaking a little. I felt awful. Whatever I'd been trying to cure by coming to Cuffs had not been cured. And even though I'd just run away from it like a scared little bunny, I knew that I missed sex.

I missed it. And I loathed it.

11

WHEN I GOT HOME, I DRANK THREE TALL GLASSES OF water and took four aspirin. Eight hours later I woke nauseated, fuzzy-headed and aching all over. *I am not hung over*, I told myself. *I am not hung over. I am not hung over.* I don't know whether I was in a deep state of denial or if I was attempting a New Age cure, but neither worked. No matter how many times I told myself I didn't have a hang over, I still did.

Maybe I should have stayed home longer, but Sundays were actually pretty busy days at Pinx Video. People did their errands on Sundays and the Mayfair was a few blocks away, not to mention the dry cleaners next door. It was easy to combine errands and get a lot accomplished in a short time. Renting and returning videos were tasks always on people's lists.

When I arrived, Mikey was in a lather. Missy worked Saturday nights with her best friend, Lainey. Lainey was new and still on probation. Probation was Mikey's idea, of course, and I barely paid attention to it.

"They're terrible together," he said. "They do nothing but gossip with each other, barely paying any attention to the customers."

"How do you know that? Did you send in a spy?" I asked. He wasn't above that.

"A friend happened to stop by. My friends know the store is important to me, and they call me when—"

"So it's a spy network?"

He pursed his lips at me. "There was a line and it took forever to check out, and the girls were giggling every time someone rented a porno."

"That's a lot of giggling."

"And look at that," he said, waving at the end of the counter. "They didn't even take out the trash."

I didn't get too upset about the trash, Missy had told me she didn't like to go out behind the building at night. It frightened her. I did probably need to ask her not to giggle when the customers rented porn, though. That was a no-no.

"They're both on this week, Friday and Saturday?"

He nodded.

"I'll come in both nights for a couple of hours just to make my presence known. How about that?"

"It's a start."

"And I'll take the trash out," I said.

"No! You have five employees, you shouldn't be taking the trash out. You should *never* take out the trash." Sometimes, he was just as protective of me as he was of the store. It was one of the things that made him tolerable.

He pulled the plastic bag of trash out of the tall plastic waste bin and tied it off. There was the strong smell of day-old Thai food in the air. Missy and Lainey must have ordered in. I'd told them to each take a half an hour lunch one after the other, but they always ate lunch together behind the counter and tried to get paid through lunch. I'd stood on my head trying to get them not to do it, but the girls didn't understand annoying little things like labor laws.

Mikey walked by me and went out the back. I looked out at the store and noted there were seven customers browsing the shelves.

A woman of about thirty-five, still wearing her aerobics outfit, came up to the counter and asked, "Do you have *Batman Returns*? My nephew really wants to see it."

"Actually, that's not even in theaters yet."

"Oh, I know, June nineteenth. You don't have any under-the-counter copies, do you?"

"No, we don't have *any* under-the-counter videos."

"Really?"

Some video places did have under-the counter-videos. They were videos that had been pirated, leaked by studio vendors or their employees. They were almost always incomplete with whole scenes still in green screen. I couldn't imagine why anyone would watch—

Mikey came running back into the store. "Noah, Noah, there's somebody in the dumpster. Dead."

I said, "Excuse me," to the woman trying to rent illegal videos for her nephew and walked out the back of the store. There was a green metal garbage dumpster in the small parking lot we shared with the dry cleaner and Taco Maria.

The dumpster was shoved up against the back of the building. It sat on wheels about six inches off the ground and was about four feet deep. That meant the rim of the container was almost at eye level. It was picked up on Mondays and Thursdays, and was nearly full. Most of the garbage came from Taco Maria's. And most of it had been sitting there all weekend.

I stood on my tippy-toes to get a good look and saw that a man's body was sprawled atop the garbage, almost like a garnish on a plate of enchiladas. He lay face down, so I couldn't see who it was. He did look dead, though.

I went back into the store and found Mikey checking out the woman who'd wanted *Batman Returns*. She was renting *Hudson Hawk* and *Robin Hood*, probably two of the worst movies from the year before. In my book, she was getting what she deserved.

"Did you call the police?" I whispered into Mikey's ear.

He shook his head.

"Okay, I'll do it." I went over to the phone and dialed 911. When the dispatcher came on the line, I said, "This is Pinx Video store on Hyperion. We have a dead body in the garbage container behind the store. Could you send someone out?"

I was ridiculously calm, probably because Mikey was freaking out for me. He finished checking the *Batman Returns* woman out, then turned to me. "Oh my God! How long do you think there's been a body out there?"

"Not long. A few hours maybe."

"How can you tell?" he asked.

"There's no garbage on him. If he was dumped there last night before Taco Maria's closed he'd be under a couple of big bags of Mexican food gone wrong."

"Do you think it has something to do with Taco Maria's? Was he Mexican? I didn't get a good look."

"I couldn't see very well and he's face down, but I think he's white. His hair is kind of a light brown."

"Probably a homeless person. They're always getting themselves killed." That seemed to make him feel better, though I had no idea why.

"We should probably close the store," I said.

"What? No. Sunday is always one of our best days."

"I think we're going to be crawling with policemen in just a few minutes."

And just on cue, we heard a siren coming closer and closer. Mikey looked at me and said, "This is going to be awful, isn't it?"

"Yes, I think so."

"Let's start with this," Javier O'Shea said. "Why is Guy Peterson's body in your dumpster?"

Of course, I should have known it was Guy in the dumpster. I knew that he had light brown, sandy hair, and I knew that people wanted him dead. I mean, people who knew he was alive wanted him dead. And maybe that's why I didn't think it was him right off. I assumed there weren't enough people who knew he was alive.

"I don't have any idea what Guy's doing in the dumpster," I said, quite honestly.

"Did you know that he was alive?" O'Shea asked.

We were crammed into my small office. O'Shea sitting in my chair behind the desk, Nino Percy leaning against the wall hulking over me, and little ole me in the guest chair. I had a split second to decide whether to tell the truth or not. If I told them everything they could easily get to my apartment, find the photos, destroy them and, eventually, I'd end up in a different dumpster in another part of the city.

"No. Did you?"

"What is that supposed to mean?" Percy asked. I didn't like the anger in his eyes. Or the contempt.

"You're the ones who've been investigating Guy Peterson, wouldn't you be more likely to know he's alive? Was alive. Whatever."

"Don't be a smart ass. Smart asses are always guilty."

"I wasn't being a smart ass. I was making a valid point. It's only logical that you'd know more about this than I do."

"Not if you're the killer. I have a bad feeling about you."

I had a bad feeling about Nino Percy, but it didn't seem a good idea to say so.

"Your car was seen in the parking lot last night after midnight," Percy said.

"Yes, I parked it there when I went to a bar down the street. I got a little drunk last night."

I glanced at O'Shea. *Did his partner know he was in Detour last night?* I wondered.

"Did anyone see you at this bar?" Percy asked.

"Well, it was full of people, so, yes."

"Anyone you can name?"

I glanced at O'Shea who was being far too quiet. I didn't like what was going on. They could put me at the spot where the body was found, probably somewhere around the time it was dumped. In fact, the body probably was dumped while I was down at Cuffs. And, if they figured out Guy was in my apartment just the night before…

There was already more so-called evidence against me than I liked.

I stared at Percy for a second and said, "I think I'd like to call my lawyer."

"We're not arresting you," O'Shea said.

"Good. I'd still like to call my lawyer." I reached over my desk and picked up my address book. "I get a phone call, right?"

"After," Percy said. "You get a lawyer and a phone call *after* we read you your rights."

"That sounds like you're telling me I can't make a phone call right now. But, see, if you haven't arrested me, I can make as many phone calls to as many lawyers as I want. Isn't that true?"

It was, so neither of them said anything.

I opened my address book to the page that had the number of the attorney who'd helped me with Jeffer's family, Franklin Carlotto. I smiled at them while I dialed.

"Hello?" It was Marc on the other end. I'd dialed their number from memory and on purpose.

"Yes, Mrs. Carlotto. Sorry to bother you on a Sunday."

"I think you have the wrong number," Marc said.

"This is Noah Valentine. Can I speak to your husband?"

"Okay. What's going on?"

I waited. Smiling at O'Shea and Percy. "This will just take a minute," I whispered to them. Legally, I'm sure I could have asked them to leave the room. They knew that. They didn't have any right to listen to my half of a conversation with my lawyer. And that meant they weren't going to budge unless asked. My whole idea, though, was to have them listen.

"Franklin, yes. Listen, a dead body was found in the dumpster behind the store this morning and I'm here with the police."

"Oh shit," Marc said. "Was it Guy Peterson?"

"Yes, it is *very* distressing."

"You need us to do something, don't you?" Marc guessed. "But you're not alone."

"That's right. As I said I'm here with the police and I want to make sure of something. I don't have to talk to them if I don't want to, do I?"

"I have no idea," Marc admitted.

"I do, I do want to be cooperative. But if I feel like I might be a suspect…uh-huh, uh-huh…"

"Oh," Marc said, suddenly getting it. "If you're a suspect, they'll search your apartment."

"Uh-huh…"

"You want us to go upstairs and get the photographs." He was very good at this game.

"Yes, I understand. He was an acquaintance. I didn't know him well."

"Ah, and we should maybe wipe down the window Guy crawled through in case there are fingerprints."

"Yes, all right. Well, thank you."

"Come to dinner later," Marc said. "Provided you're not in jail."

"All right, well, thank you very much."

I hung up and looked at the two detectives. "So, as I said to my lawyer, I'm happy to cooperate unless I feel like I'm a suspect at which point we stop talking."

"Listen, you snotty little fag—" Percy started, but O'Shea was out of his chair pushing his partner out of the room. They had a classic good cop/bad cop thing going, but it wasn't working too well.

After about a minute, O'Shea came back in.

"Sorry about that. He's a little passionate at times."

"He's a bully."

He shrugged. "We deal with bullies." He left the idea that sometimes you have to be the bigger bully unspoken. Of course, if you weren't a member of the LAPD the 'sometimes' seemed a lot more like *all* the time.

"So, after you saw me at Detour, you went to Cuffs."

That stopped me. I'd never said the name of the bar. Should I ignore it or should tell him? I felt safer with O'Shea, but that's not the same as feeling safe.

"Yes, I went to Cuffs. I stood outside in the line for about fifteen minutes. Then I got in. I wasn't there very long. Maybe twenty minutes."

"And you didn't see anyone you knew."

"No."

"Why didn't you stay longer?"

"Because I didn't see anyone I knew."

"You didn't go there to see people you know. That's not why people go to Cuffs, is it?"

"How do you know? Last night I was explaining how guys connect. Now you know what goes on at Cuffs?"

"I know all the gay bars in Rampart. I don't know the specifics, I guess, the details. But I have a pretty good idea what goes on in this neighborhood and where it goes on."

"We're not doing anything illegal."

"That's not entirely true. There's a lot of drugs being bought and sold, a healthy trade in male prostitution, and occasionally you guys kill each other. Or manage to get yourselves killed."

He kind of had a point. A homicide detective in this neighborhood would need to know at least a little about the bars. Maybe this was why he knew where I went without my having to say.

"Did you go home after Cuffs?" he asked.

"Yes."

"You do see that Guy Peterson's body showing up in your dumpster is suspicious."

"Except for one thing. If I killed Guy Peterson I would have left his body somewhere else. Don't you think?"

12

We weren't able to reopen for the rest of the day. After they spoke to me and to Mikey, Percy and O'Shea went out to the dumpster and we locked up the store.

Before going home, Mikey and I stood at the edge of the back parking lot. The sky was thick and steel-colored, it was just over seventy degrees as it had been for days. That seemed somehow appropriate for staring at a crime scene. Bright and sunny would have felt wrong. Mikey and I watched with our arms tightly crossed.

Three guys wearing dark blue windbreakers with the letters SID on the back were carefully taking everything out of the dumpster bit by bit and examining it. It had to be disgusting work.

They'd set up a white tent with no sides next to the dumpster. The body lay underneath it on a plastic sheet. Another guy wore the same kind of blue jacket except his said CORONER on the back. He was attached to the white van parked in front of Pinx Video. He leaned over the body and made notes.

Guy had been turned face up and even from thirty feet away I could see there was a large bloodstain on his shirt.

"He was either shot or stabbed," I said to Mikey.

"Shot."

"How do you know that?"

"Detective Percy asked if you owned a gun."

They didn't ask me if I owned a gun.

"What did you tell them?" I asked.

"That you don't keep a gun at Pinx. I mean, I have no idea if you have a gun at home."

"I don't have a gun at home. Guns scare me. You know that. You could have told them that."

"If I talk to them again, I will."

We watched for a bit. Percy and O'Shea stood around looking unhappy. Every so often a uniformed officer came over to speak to them. I imagined that uniforms were going around the neighborhood asking questions about last night.

"My car was in the parking lot just after midnight. I left it here while I was down at Cuffs," I told Mikey.

"Really? I knew you had to be into something, but I didn't think it was that."

"I don't—never mind. Did they say anything about that? About my car being here?"

"No."

"I wonder how they knew?"

The lot was set down about five feet below the sidewalk. To enter it you came down a short ramp. To leave you went up another ramp. There was room for about twelve cars and we shared the lot with the dry cleaners and Taco Mario. We didn't encourage our customers to use the lot, it was too small.

Mikey glanced up at a two-story apartment building behind the parking lot to the east, and then at another behind me to the south. A lot of people could have seen my car. But then, they would have only seen a red Sentra and the city was full of them. How did they know it was mine?

"What else did they ask you about?"

"What kind of person you were. I told them you were nice."

"Thank you for lying."

"I didn't—oh, that's a joke. Sorry, I'm still kind of freaked. They asked how well you knew Guy Peterson. You didn't know him well, did you? I mean, you seemed like you didn't."

"I didn't know him well." Something occurred to me. "Did you tell them about Guy's boyfriend?"

"I did. Should I have not done that?"

"No, Mikey, you did fine. Telling the truth is never the wrong thing to do."

It was an awkward thing to say. I was hardly following my own advice. I'd lied to the police but only because I thought they might kill me. I didn't think they'd kill Mikey, so it was fine that he'd told the truth. For him. It might not work out so well for Ted Bain.

"So, who was it that died in the camera shop?" Mikey asked.

"I have no idea. I heard there are still over a hundred people missing after the riots. I guess whoever it is, they're on that list."

A few minutes later, we went back into the store. I told Mikey he should go home and pay himself for a full day. Even if the police finished soon I didn't see much point in reopening. I hung around to call the evening shift and tell them not to come in, and locked up.

I was almost finished when I realized there was one more thing I needed to do. I signed in to the computer system, which had been the most expensive part of opening the store, though it did save me the nightmare of doing things by hand.

The first screen came up and I got four options: New Sale, New Record, Reports, Record Look Up. I clicked on Record Look Up. That brought me to a screen with the choices Customer and Video. There I chose Customer. That brought up a screen with all of the same fields that came up when you entered a new customer. Except on this page you enter the last name or some portion of the last name. I typed in B-A-I-N. The first record that came up was for a woman named Tanya Bain. I hit Return and the next screen came up. That was BAIN, TED. His information immediately filled in, including his address, 648 N. Lafayette, and his phone number.

The counter phone was right next to me, so I'd dialed before I really thought things through.

"Hello?"

The moment Ted answered I realized something important;

he probably didn't know that Guy had been killed. I was going to have to be the one to tell him.

"Hello? Guy?"

"No. Um, Noah Valentine from the video store."

"Oh. I was afraid of this. I can't talk to you. You really need to stop being so damned nosey."

"Guy is dead."

"Yes, Guy is dead. I know that. He's been dead for more than a week."

"They found his body in dumpster behind the video store. You knew he didn't die in the fire, that's why you thought he was calling you."

"I need to lie down."

"Don't go, not yet. The police know who you are."

"What?! Oh my God!"

"Ted, tell me what's going on. Why was Guy afraid of the police? Why are you afraid of the police?"

"I feel sick. Guy is really dead? This isn't a trick?"

"Guy is really dead. Tell me what's going on so I can help you."

"I have to go. I have to find some place safe."

"Do you have a friend you can stay with?"

"I think so. I have to go—"

"Call me tomorrow. Let me know you're okay."

"Why would I do that?"

"Because, I think I just saved your life."

When I walked into the courtyard, Marc was setting the table. "There you are! Go freshen up, we're having company."

"Oh, no, I don't want to intrude," I said. "We can talk later. The police didn't come by and search my—"

"Not yet. I've already set you a place. I want hear all about Guy Peterson's second death."

"Well, all right."

"Good. Deborah and Rob are coming."

I walked up the stairs wondering if I shouldn't wait until later on to catch Marc and Louis up. Marc worked with Deborah at the studio. I'd met her before. I'd met *them* before. She was short and a little chunky with thick brown hair cut into boyish layers. He was vastly taller, pale, with nearly translucent skin. They were nice enough but as bland as unbuttered toast.

Upstairs, I threw on a chambray shirt, khaki shorts and a pair of Pumas. I struggled fruitlessly with my hair, and spritzed myself with Antaeus. I was about to go downstairs when the phone rang. I picked up.

"Weren't you going to call me?"

"I'm sorry, Mom, there's a lot going on."

"Really? Tell me."

Goddammit, I thought, I didn't actually want to tell her what was going on. 'Gee, Mom, the police think I'm a murderer' wasn't something you told your mother on—

"Oh my God, it's Mother's Day, isn't it?"

"It is."

"I should have sent you flowers."

"Oh, now, you're a busy young man, I'm sure you were doing something else equally important."

"Well, I wish I'd taken the time to do it."

"So, is the city recovering from the riots? You know people here are still talking about it."

"Are they?"

"They don't understand how people could just destroy their own neighborhoods."

"It's anger. And I'm glad your friends don't understand it. People shouldn't understand that kind of anger."

"Well, that's an interesting way to look at it. I'll have to think about that." She seemed a little annoyed that I might be disagreeing with her. "Now, I know you don't want to talk about this, but have you met any nice young men?"

"You're right. I don't want to talk about it."

"Have you thought about going to church?" she asked. "Patty Baird down the street told me her son, you remember him, Donald? Well Donald goes to a church in San Francisco that accepts gays. So you must have something like that in Los Angeles. Seriously, we're all sinners, I don't know why some people get so upset about who's committing which sin. Or a club! You could join a club."

"Speaking of which, how's the garden club?" I asked, my usual way of distracting her. She could talk for hours about the garden club, its politics were as cutthroat and ruthless as Washington's. Every time I talked to her about it I was surprised that anything got planted at all. Or weeded. Or watered.

After I'd let her go on for a few minutes, I interrupted and said, "I need to go, Mom. I'm having Sunday dinner with my neighbors."

"The boys downstairs, I take it. You spend too much time with them. You'll never meet anyone hanging around a couple."

"Yes, Mom. I'll talk to you next week."

Before I could forget, I dialed 411 and asked the operator for the number of The Flower Children, the florist near Sunset and Silver Lake Boulevards. For an extra twenty-five cents she connected me. Already in their computer, I ordered the same arrangement they'd sent my mother last year and paid extra for it to arrive by Tuesday.

A minute or two after I hung up, I stuck my head into Marc and Louis' apartment, which was like mine though they'd done a better job decorating. Their living room had four comfortable chairs in a conversational square, a café table in the dining area and not much else, besides a stereo. There was a TV and VCR in the bedroom, but I don't think they ever used it.

I said, "Hello?"

Marc came out of the kitchen with a glass of white wine saying, "There you are! I poured this for you ages ago."

Louis came out wearing an apron that had a picture of a bodybuilder's body on it. "Marc tells me they found Guy Peterson's body. Again."

"In the dumpster behind Pinx."

"They returned him like an overdue video."

"Oh, Louis."

"What about Mr. Crispy, have they figured out who he was?"

"No, I don't think so."

"The photographs are in the bedroom closet, and we wiped down all your windows and doors," Marc said.

"You might want to touch everything so it doesn't look like we did that," suggested Louis.

"How was Guy killed?" Marc asked.

"Gunshot. Or at least it looked like a gunshot from a distance. And the police asked Mikey if I had a gun."

"They think you did it?"

"Of course they do," Louis said. "Why else are you and I hiding and destroying evidence?"

"Noah didn't kill anyone so it's not evidence of anything."

"Tell that to the police."

"Are you sure you want me here for Sunday dinner? I mean, I don't want to dominate the conversation."

"You're fine," Louis said. "Some conversations deserve to be dominated."

"Yoo-hoo, hello?"

"Speak of the devil," Louis said.

We filed out of the apartment to meet them and I immediately saw that it was Deborah, Rob and someone else. A young man of around twenty-four, even taller than Rob, with a very prominent Adam's apple and a chin that must have gone into the witness protection program. I scolded myself for judging him solely on his looks. He did have pretty eyes, though not pretty enough to make up for the sinking feeling I was getting in my stomach.

"Louis, Marc, *No-ah*," Deborah said. "This is my brother, Jamie. He's visiting from St. Louis but thinking of moving to California, so let's put our best foot forward."

"I don't have a best foot. My feet are always misbehaving," Louis said. Deborah slapped him lightly on the upper arm, then everyone said hello and Marc ran off to get drinks. Louis followed to check on dinner, Deborah and Rob trailed after him pointedly leaving me alone with Jamie.

We smiled uncomfortably at each other until he said, "Deborah says you own a video store."

"I do."

"I'd love to see it."

"Um, well, it's closed right now."

"On a Sunday? Really? In St. Louis video stores are open seven days a week."

"Yes, well, we found a dead body this morning in the dumpster behind the building."

"Oh my God," he said. "Did you know this person?"

"Yes, as a matter of fact I did know him. But we weren't close."

"Still. Who do they think did it?"

"Well, me at the moment. I'm hoping they'll get over that."

Deborah and Rob came out of the apartment holding large glasses of chilled white wine. "Louis kicked us out of his kitchen," Rob said, trying something that was almost a smile.

"How are you two getting along?" Deborah asked, sipping her wine. I was right; it was a fix-up. But hopefully I'd just put the quash on that.

"Noah is a murder suspect," Jamie said with some obvious delight.

Deborah nearly spit her wine out. "Oh, he is not. Noah would never kill someone."

Why she'd think that, I had no idea. We'd probably spent a total of ten hours together spread over a year and a half. I'm sure I was polite, but that's no reason to think me incapable of murder.

"I didn't say he *was* a killer. I said he was a *suspect*." Then he turned to me and said, "Of course I might be wrong. Did you kill him, Noah?"

"That's a tricky question," I said. "If I were a killer I'd lie and say I wasn't. Which is the same answer I'd give if I weren't a killer. So how can you be sure?"

"If they had any proof, you'd be in jail right now," Deborah said.

"We found the body about four hours ago."

Night Drop

"Oh, I see," she said, realizing I could very well be a murderer.

Louis came out with a platter of cheese and crackers. "Here's a little something so no one starves to death." He set the big dish on the table and said, "Sit, sit. Has Noah been telling you he's public enemy number one?"

"You shouldn't joke, Louis," Deborah admonished him, as we took seats. Jamie sat next to me, smiling at me as he did. *Oh God*, I thought. *A dead body and a blind date on the same day.* It was giving me a headache. Or had my hangover not gone away?

"So?" Marc said, looking at me. "What don't we know?"

"Someone killed Guy Peterson and threw him in the dumpster behind Pinx."

"So, it's someone who knows you knew Guy. I mean, you don't think it's random that they picked *your* dumpster, do you?"

"No, I don't think so."

"So, who knows that you know Guy?"

"Well, I think pretty much everyone we suspected the first time Guy died."

"The first time?" Deborah asked. "People don't die more than once."

"He owned a camera shop which burned during the riots and there was a body inside—"

"Mr. Crispy."

"Louis' pet name for the corpse," Marc explained. "Anyway, everyone thought he was Guy Peterson."

"Guy's father identified the body," I added.

"Can you even do that?" Deborah asked. "If the body's been burned?"

"Sure," Rob said. "Tattoos, scars, general appearance. And bodies aren't always completely burned. It's often partial." I had no idea what Rob did for a living or why he might know those things.

"Obviously, whoever killed Mr. Crispy killed Guy Peterson," Louis said.

"Why is that obvious?" Marc asked. "Maybe Guy killed Mr. Crispy and that's *why* he got killed."

"Or maybe Guy's death had nothing to do with Mr. Crispy?" I said.

"Maybe we should talk about something else," Deborah said. "Dead people make for terrible dinner conversation."

Actually, I didn't mind a change of subject. I turned to Jamie and asked, "How do you like St. Louis?"

"Living there is like being in a persistent vegetative state."

Comas were a step up from death, but they made for terrible dinner conversation, too.

Deborah spent several minutes insisting that St. Louis was a wonderful city and she'd move back in a minute if it weren't for Rob's work.

"What do you do, Rob?" I asked.

"I work for the Arboretum."

"Oh, they don't have plants in St. Louis?"

"Not these plants," he said.

"Rob's an expert on yuccas," Deborah said proudly.

I resisted the temptation to say, 'Yuck.' It wasn't easy.

Then, thankfully, it was time for dinner. Louis had made a delicious leg of lamb that he served with scalloped potatoes and homemade mint jelly. Dessert was a coconut cream pie from a bakery somewhere on the East Side that he steadfastly refused to reveal.

During dinner Deborah and Rob talked about their fears about buying a home. Rob wanted to, but Deborah was sure that prices would fall further. He said that wouldn't matter if they stayed in the house for ten years, but she just couldn't imagine staying for more than five due to their imaginary and as yet unconceived children.

Before desert I excused myself and went upstairs to use the bathroom. I'd only eaten a little at dinner, but I drank too much wine, which, after the day before, was a terrible idea. I spent some much needed time in the bathroom, washed my hands and face. I looked mournfully at my hair, which resembled a bunch of chocolate kisses doing a conga line, and was about to go back downstairs when I realized I could hear a conversation floating up from the living room directly below me.

"I thought you said he was a nice guy," Deborah said.

"He is a nice guy," Marc replied.

"A nice guy who's a murder suspect."

"I wouldn't take that seriously."

"You said his lover died. Do you know how?"

"I don't know the exact circumstances. He doesn't like to talk about it."

"So there could be a pattern?"

"Oh my God, Deborah! You're being ridiculous."

"We're talking about my brother. I just want Jamie to be safe."

"I promise, Noah will not kill your brother. Okay?"

"I don't *think* he's a murderer but…"

"But? That's not the kind of sentence you end with a but."

"Innocent people don't get involved with murder. I don't want to see my brother corrupted."

"Did I miss something? Is your brother a virgin in a Harlequin novel?"

"Marc! I'm being serious and you're making fun of me."

"Look, it's really not up to you. Or me. Or anyone except the two of them. And, in case you're not paying attention, they don't seem to be hitting it off."

"What do you mean? You don't think Noah likes Jamie?"

"I don't think he likes him in the way you're worried about."

"He'd be lucky to go out with Jamie."

"You don't want them to go out, remember?"

"But I don't want my brother to be rejected."

I'd had enough. I needed to go back downstairs and quickly think of an excuse to leave. *An emergency at the video store?* I wondered. But we didn't really have emergencies at Pinx. And besides, I already told everyone we'd closed for the day.

I got back downstairs and found Jamie alone at the table. Marc and Deborah were still in the house, I could almost hear them continuing to argue. Rob was giving Louis a lecture on a couple of succulents at the far end of the courtyard.

"I'm sorry," Jamie said. "I didn't know she was going to do this. I mean, she mentioned you. And that it would be nice if we met. I just, I know this is a bad time."

"It's not the worst thing that's happened to me recently."

"You know they're in there fighting about us," he said.

"I know. Please don't take any of this personally. I'm not really—"

"Don't worry," he said, leaning forward. "I'm not the white picket fence kind of guy my sister wants me to be."

"Ah."

He lowered his voice and asked, "Do you know where the sex clubs are?"

I almost laughed. "Well, there's one a couple blocks that way and two or three just north of here on Sunset. The best thing to do is pick up a copy of *Frontiers*. Look at the ads in the back."

"And where do I get that?"

"Any gay business." As soon as I said I realized an out-of-towner might not recognize a gay business when he saw one. "A Different Light. Bookstore. It's on Santa Monica, near San Vincente, I think."

"Oh, do they have porn? You know, like *Mandate*, *Honcho*, *Inches*. I can get *Playgirl* in St. Louis, but it's so boring."

"Circus of Books is better for that. There's one just down the street from A Different Light. And there's one over here on Sunset. They're both pretty cruisy."

"Oh, perfect."

One of the nice things about being an Angelino was helping tourists. Actually, Jamie seemed like a nice kid and I had a moment of guilt about judging a man by his chin.

13

THE NEXT MORNING AT ABOUT SEVEN, THERE WAS A KNOCK on my door. I wasn't usually out of bed before nine so I was not especially excited. When I opened the door, Marc and Louis stood there with a pitcher of orange juice, a bag of Brooklyn Bagels and a giant tub of cream cheese. Marc had a couple of newspapers tucked under his arm. They were both dressed for the office.

"Long time no see," I said.

"We found Mr. Crispy," Louis said.

That left me no choice but to let them in—though I was sorely tempted slam the door in their faces.

"You do have a toaster, don't you?"

"Of course I have a toaster. You've been in my kitchen, Louis, you know what's there."

"And a coffeemaker?"

I sighed. "Next to the toaster."

Louis went into the kitchen. Marc laid the newspapers on the dining table; one was the *LA Times* and the other a *Frontiers* magazine from early April. He unfolded the *LA Times* and pointed to a front-page article at the bottom of the page.

RAMPART DETECTIVE MISSING

From the kitchen, I heard Louis say, "Oh my." He stuck his head out. "Marc go downstairs and grind some beans. I forgot, all he has is Maxwell House."

"Oh no, that won't do," Marc said and walked out of the apartment. Louis went back to working the toaster. I stood there blurry-eyed, reading the newspaper.

One Detective Timothy Gaines, aged 37, had been missing since the second day of the riots. His family was getting anxious —no kidding—but still hoped he'd come home safe. He'd worked out of the Rampart Division for ten years, was well-liked and deeply involved with the Frontier Scout's Trailblazer program that allows teenagers to explore careers in law enforcement.

It wasn't a long article, but then what was there to say? A man was missing after the riots. I leaned on the corner of my desk so I could talk to Louis while he sliced bagels and crammed them into my toaster. I could hear Mark grinding beans downstairs.

"It's Mr. Crispy," Louis said. "It has to be."

"The timing is right. And it fits with Guy being afraid of the police."

"And why he went into hiding. If he killed Mr. Crispy, that is."

"Gaines. If you're convinced he's Mr. Crispy you should call him Mr. Gaines. Or Tim if you want to be on a first-name basis."

Marc came in holding a baggie full of freshly ground coffee, which he handed off to Louis. To me he said, "Did you read it? I thought the part about the Trailblazers was interesting."

"Was it?"

"Oh, I haven't told you yet," he said. "So, remember that I thought those photos looked familiar?"

"The artsy ones?"

"Yes. I went back a few issues of *Frontiers*."

"He has an entire year in the bottom of the closet."

"Shut up, Louis. Anyway, I went back a few issues and I saw it." He'd flipped to the right page in *Frontiers*. "Guy Peterson was supposed to have an exhibit at the Cox Gallery on Vermont."

I looked at the article, which featured a picture in the style of the beating photos but not one of the ones I had. The name of the exhibit was *To Pummel and to Slay*. A play on the LAPD motto To Protect and to Serve.

"You said, supposed to?" I asked. "He was *supposed* to have an exhibit?"

"We drove by there on the way to get the bagels," Louis said, as he brought out a plate of toasted bagels and set them on the table. "And there's no Guy Peterson exhibit going on. None."

He set down cups of coffee in front of me and Marc. I took a sip. It tasted like coffee to me. I tried to back up a little. "So, Timothy Gaines—"

"Mr. Crispy," Louis said from the kitchen.

"Louis."

"Gaines was involved with the Trailblazers. And Guy's photos have Frontier Scouts beating a guy. What does that mean?"

"I don't know," replied Marc. "But I think it means something. It connects."

"'How,' is the question," Louis said, sitting down with his coffee.

"So, do we think Guy Peterson killed Detective Timothy Gaines?"

"He disappeared at the right time," I said.

"But that's all we know for sure," Marc pointed out.

"Don't be such a killjoy," Louis said.

"He could be up in Big Bear for all we know. And the body in Guy's Camera could be a homeless person who broke in to stay warm."

"But you thought the Trailblazers connection was interesting."

"It is. If it's not a coincidence."

"I'm not sure I like this logical side of you," Louis said.

"Mikey, my employee, told the police about Ted Bain. I called Ted and warned him. Actually, I ended up being the one to tell him Guy was dead."

"Oh, that doesn't sound fun."

"So where is he now?"

"I don't know. He didn't tell me where he was going."

"Did he tell you anything?"

"No, he was too upset."

"I'll bet he knows how this all connects."

"Yes, I'll bet he does."

"So why haven't the police searched your place yet? Are you no longer a suspect?"

"Um, I don't know. You have to get a search warrant from a judge, so you need some legitimate reason to suspect someone. Maybe they don't have enough to get a search warrant."

"This orange juice needs champagne," Marc said.

"Yeah, we have to leave for work soon," Louis pointed out.

"Oh well, one more reason to get rich."

"You know who else might know how all this connects? Whoever owns that gallery."

———

After they left, I called Mikey at home and told him I might not come into the store. He tried to contain his excitement but failed. Then I went back to sleep. Almost three hours later, I managed to drag myself out of bed for a second time. I showered, dressed, made my hair look less like a topiary, ate the half of my bagel I didn't eat at breakfast, and left the apartment.

In the car, I put in my cassette of *Miss Saigon* and sang along to "The American Dream." The song finished as I pulled up to a meter on Vermont below Franklin.

Cox Gallery sat along a stretch that had a number of artsy

little shops across from the post office. It was a narrow shop with two very large plate glass windows at the front, where two paintings—oil or acrylic I couldn't tell—of desert vistas were on display.

At least I think they were desert vistas. They were both designed with washed out blues and browns. One of them had a slash down the middle that might have been a cactus.

When I walked in, the place was deadly still. A woman sat at a desk in the back; she barely moved. An eye might have flickered when I walked in, I couldn't tell. As I got closer she did move though. She stood up and I could see that she was very thin, very tall. She wore hoop earrings and a small, cream-colored shell dress with a thin, white cardigan. I had the odd feeling her deepest desire was to be as abstract as the paintings in the window.

"Are you looking for something specific?"

"Actually, I came in to talk with the owner," I said.

She smiled. "I noticed you didn't look at the paintings. Most people look at the paintings when they come in, no matter why they're here."

I glanced at the paintings. They didn't look much different than the ones in the front.

"I'm Alicia Cox," she said.

I tried not to smile too big. Her name was a like a drag queen's. "You knew Guy Peterson?"

"Knew?"

"He was found dead," I said.

"The riots? The news has been overwhelming. I couldn't take it anymore, so I stopped paying attention."

"He was found yesterday. I don't know if it's been in the news yet. He was scheduled to have an exhibit here?"

"Yes, it should have started a few days ago. That's why—" She waved around the gallery. "I'll be honest, these aren't very good. They were all I could get on short notice."

"So, did you cancel or did Guy?"

"It was me, I'm afraid. A couple of policemen came by."

"Nino Percy and Javier O'Shea?" I asked.

"Percy sounds familiar. I don't remember the other one's name."

"Did they threaten you?"

"No. Not at all."

"Then why did you cancel the exhibit?"

"They came and said things about Guy. They said it wasn't his work, that he'd stolen it from someone. They mentioned a name, I don't remember it. They claimed it was his work Peterson was passing off as his own."

"And you believed them."

"Of course not. But then they asked about the windows. They asked if I'd ever had any problem with vandals. I said I hadn't. They said I was lucky. That windows get broken all the time. Then the taller one asked how I liked living in Beachwood Canyon and was I worried about the high instance of rape on Glen Holly," she smiled wryly. "I live on Glen Holly."

"You said they didn't threaten you."

"Well, they didn't, did they? Even if I could prove what they said, they hadn't really said anything."

"How did Guy react?"

"He was upset. Rightly so. But I'm in this to sell things to rich people, not to get hurt."

At least she was honest about it. "Do you know how the police found out about the exhibit?"

"I'm not sure, but I assume...a press release had gone out, there was a photo in the *Weekly*."

"And *Frontiers*."

"Ah, I wasn't sure."

"Why do you think the police wanted the exhibit shut down?"

"Because the photos are true."

"No, they're not. They're obviously staged."

"Yes, you're right. But they're also true."

14

I TOOK A FEW MORE STABS AT GETTING A BETTER ANSWER from Alicia Cox, but all she would say was that it was Guy who told her the photos were 'true.' And that that was half the reason she decided to show them. I couldn't decide whether he was being artistic with the comment, certainly there was 'truth' in all art, or whether there was more to the message he wanted the photos to convey. The most obvious connection was the Rodney King beating. But that didn't seem strong enough to shut the exhibit down.

Driving north on Vermont, I turned at Los Feliz. I took *Miss Saigon* out of the cassette player and put in *Les Miz*. I'd seen *Les Miz* at the Schubert in Century City with Jeffer. I'd thought it was terrible, though, I still liked the music. Actually a little better than *Miss Saigon*.

Driving down Los Feliz, I glanced over at Guy's building and noticed his mother and father standing next to some kind of dusty Ford truck with an extended cab, parked illegally. Cindy was walking out of the building carrying a plastic pail with a mop sticking out of it.

I screeched to halt and parked in front of the building, also illegally. Just in case, I put my flashers on before I ran over to the Peterson's.

"Hello."

"What do you want?" Cindy said, putting down the bucket. I got a whiff of soapy bleach. I guessed they must really want Guy's security deposit back.

"I have a couple of questions I wanted to ask your father."

"Why should he answer them?"

"Do you care at all about what happened to your brother?"

"Of course we do. But you're not anybody. You're just the video guy."

"And somebody threw your brother into the dumpster behind my store," I said defiantly.

Guy's mother squeaked. *Well, that was nice,* I thought. *Somebody gives a crap about him.*

"Mr. Peterson, you identified the wrong body. Can you tell me how that happened?"

He seemed to shrink as he formulated his answer. "They confused me. I mean, they said it had to be Guy. I mean, the thing they showed me, with all its skin burned off... It could have been Guy. It could have been anybody."

"Who were *they*?"

"Those policeman. Percy and the other one."

"It didn't bother you not to know for sure?"

"No, it didn't. They were sure. Percy was sure, that was enough for me. And they said they was gonna do some tests."

"But you went through his things. You had a memorial."

"Stop talking to him like he's done something wrong," Cindy growled at me. "What about Guy? Huh? Where was he? Why didn't he let us know he was alive? Did you ever think of that?"

"Guy was in hiding because he thought the police were going to kill him, and you know what? They probably did."

Out of the corner of my eye, a black-and-white went buy. I ran back to my car as fast as I could. Up in front of me, the black-and-white was slowing down. He saw me get into the car and sped up. Thank God. A traffic ticket was the last thing I needed.

When I looked in the rear view mirror, I saw that the Petersons had piled into their truck and were driving away. I pulled out into traffic and drove down to the next street and turned right. A few minutes later I was on Hyperion and turning into the parking lot for Pinx Video.

The first thing that happened after I walked through the employee entrance was Mikey telling me that Lainey had quit.

"I told you not to be so hard on her," I said.

"Noah, she quit because the police were asking questions about you. Her parents wouldn't let her keep working here."

"Why did they question Lainey?"

"They've questioned everyone."

"Well, they're not going to find out anything. They're wasting their time." Of course, if they were the ones who killed Guy they would want to waste time, wouldn't they?

There were a lot of returns that needed to be input into the computer and then re-shelved. I volunteered to do that while Mikey dealt with some new videos that had come in: re-orders on *The Fisher King, Dead Again* and Madonna's *Truth or Dare.* In a second box we got new additions to the classics shelf *The Parent Trap* and *Freaky Friday.*

As I worked, I kept thinking about Guy Peterson. Was there a way to just stop all of this? A way to pull myself out of this mess? If there was I couldn't see it. It really seemed like Percy and O'Shea might be trying to pin this on me. Obviously, it wasn't going that well if they couldn't even get a search warrant, but that didn't mean the tide couldn't turn. If I did nothing they might succeed. I had to keep trying to understand what was going on, right?

I was almost finished with the input when I realized Mikey was standing next to me.

"Yes?"

"Bob Diamond called. You haven't given him all the tax information."

"Crap."

Bob Diamond, CPA was the store's accountant. He'd filed an extension for our 1991 taxes but not without a half hour lecture cataloguing all the reasons I needed to finish ASAP. It had been almost a month and I'd done almost nothing.

"You have to pay attention to things like that," Mikey said, using an embarrassingly parental tone.

"Um, I know. I've just been a little busy lately. I mean, you did notice the dead body in the dumpster yesterday."

"I'm not just talking about taxes. Noah, I know how much you're making. You really could make a lot more with just a little push."

"Okay, I need to go pull info together for Bob Diamond. I'll do it. I promise."

"Lube."

"What about lube?"

"Lube. We should sell lube. To go with the porn. One stop shopping." He gave me a look and said, "Or do you not understand how masturbation works?"

"I understand just fine. I don't know, Mikey, I mean half our customers are straight. I don't want to offend—"

"Straight people masturbate."

"Yes, I knew that."

The bell over the front door rang. I turned around to see Detective O'Shea standing there. He wore a shapeless gray sport jacket over a light blue oxford shirt and a pair of tailored jeans. He had me locked in his sights.

"What was at Cox Gallery?" he asked, when he got to the counter.

"Mikey, could you put these back on the shelves." I handed him a stack of empty cardboard video boxes. Then I waited for him to be out of earshot. "You followed me?"

"It is my job."

"Because I'm a suspect?"

"I don't know if I'd go that far. You have something to do with this, though, and I'd like to know what. What were you doing at Cox Gallery?"

"This won't come as much of a surprise. The owner told me you and Percy stopped by and made sure Guy Peterson's show got canceled. Why did you do that?"

"He's lying."

"She. The owner of the gallery is a she."

"Okay. She's lying." He frowned deeply at me. "So, Peterson was supposed to have an exhibit there but it got canceled? Why do you think that's important?"

I decided not to answer. I wasn't sure if it was safe to talk to him about the photos. Actually, I wasn't sure it was safe to talk to him at all.

"Did you see me talking to the Petersons?"

"You should maybe leave them alone. They're grieving."

"You coerced Mr. Peterson into saying Mr. Crispy was Guy when he clearly wasn't."

He smirked. "Mr. Crispy. That's dark. Funny, but dark. You could have been a cop. You've got the gallows humor down." I decided not to tell him it was Louis' joke.

"And what about Detective Gaines?" I asked.

"What about him?"

"He's missing. Have you checked to see if he's Mr. Crispy? Could the body from the camera store be Gaines?"

He was very thoughtful for a moment. "Gaines was Nino's regular partner. How did you know Gaines is missing?"

"It was in the newspaper."

"Oh. I've been a little busy. I didn't know they'd released that information. You know this isn't how this is supposed to work."

"What do you mean?"

"I think I've asked three questions and you've asked about ten," he said.

It wasn't *that* bad. Though, I will admit to being an inquisitive sort.

He took a good long, uncomfortable look at me. "We're looking for Ted Bain. Do you know where he is?"

"Why? Why are you looking for him?"

"No. The way this works is, I ask a question and then you answer it. Where is he?"

He waited. When I didn't say anything, he said, "You know things you're not telling me."

"I could say the same about you."

"Where is Ted Bain?"

"I'm not saying anything about Ted Bain, unless you tell me why you're looking for him."

"You have to trust me," he said, his puppy dog eyes looking extra sincere.

"No, I don't."

Actually, I really wanted to know where Ted Bain was myself. It had only been twenty-four hours since I'd tipped him off that the police knew about him, but I'd have appreciated a phone call. I wondered how I might find him.

After Detective O'Shea left I took a stab at organizing the accounts in my windowless office. It was an effort that didn't last long. I went back up to the front and checked out customers until there was a lull.

"I didn't need you," Mikey said. "It's really okay if people wait in line for a minute or two."

"Sorry," I said, apologizing for working in my own store. "You knew that Ted and Guy were boyfriends. How did you know that?"

Mikey blushed, something he almost never did. "Well, it's kind of embarrassing."

"Did you have sex with Ted?"

"No. Randy did."

"While you were together?"

He nodded. "It was a long time ago. I mean, we almost broke up, but then Ted came into the store and there I am looking at him, thinking, 'I would have sex with him in a heart-beat.' So then I couldn't be mad at Randy anymore. Except for the fact that he got to screw Ted Bain and I didn't. I still hold that over his head."

"Do you know much about Ted? Do you know any of his friends?"

"Do you want go out with him? Obviously he's single, but you should maybe wait. At least a couple of weeks."

"Seriously?"

"What?"

"Ted is hiding from the police."

"Oh. I guess that would make him hard to date."

"And I'd like to *talk* to him."

"Okay. Let me put on my thinking cap." He started to think. It made him frown.

Meanwhile, a young guy came up to the counter, so I checked him out. He was renting two Falcon Videos, *Plunge* and *The Big Ones*. Most guys rented a regular movie at the same time just so they didn't seem like complete pervs. I had to admire his boldness.

As soon as he walked away, Mikey said, "He has this close girlfriend. She lives in the same building with him. But that's all I know."

"Does she rent videos from us?"

"Yeah, I think I've seen her here."

"Let's do a look-up on his address and see if she comes up."

"We can do that?"

I was surprised he didn't know, though we usually only looked people up by name. And, I was the one who got the demo when we had the system put in.

"Yeah, you can search on any field. It was a selling point when we bought the system. Though, I don't remember needing to look anyone up by their address before."

Mikey got on the computer and quickly navigated to the correct field. He put in Ted's address on Lafayette. Two records came up. Ted's and a woman named Ivy Bell.

"Do you want to call her?" Mikey asked.

"Yes, let's."

He picked up the phone and dialed. I wondered what he was going to say if she answered, "Hello, I have Mr. Valentine calling?" or was he going to carry on the entire conversation?

Looking over his shoulder, he said, "Answering machine."

"Don't leave a message. I'll drive over."

Twenty minutes later, I was sitting outside Ted Bain's apartment building. It was a five-minute drive, but I'd had to zigzag all over the neighborhood to make sure I wasn't followed.

The building was a filthy white, slab-like affair from the late fifties. It climbed a slight hill in three separate levels. Ted and Ivy lived next door to each other in the middle level. There was no security and I only had to find the right set of stairs to reach the second floor. Ivy was in apartment D and Ted in C. I reached Ivy's door first.

I knocked. Several times. There was no answer, but then I wasn't sure I was expecting one. Before I left Pinx Video, I'd written out a brief note asking that Ted call me. I slipped it under the door.

My errand complete, curiosity led me down to apartment C. I knew Ted wouldn't be there. Still, I knocked. Well, tried to knock. As soon as my knuckles hit the door it fell open. I looked down at the doorknob and saw that someone had kicked the door open and then pulled it shut later on. The molding inside had broken and needed to be replaced. The lock was in pretty bad shape, too.

The apartment was shotgun style. There was a living room, a dining area, a kitchen you walked through to get to the bedroom in the back of the apartment. I didn't immediately see exactly where the bathroom was. I was too busy looking at the mess in front of me.

Ted Bain liked books. Looking at him you wouldn't think so. Pretty people have a reputation for not exactly being smart, so it was something of a surprise to find that the center of his living room was one gigantic pile of books. Someone had knocked over three bookcases, which had, presumably, been full. The sofa was overturned, its cushions tossed around, and the TV face down on the floor. Looking down the hallway I could see that his closet had received the same treatment, and the bedroom was littered with his clothes.

Amid the debris, I noticed that a box of headshots had been opened and dumped so that there were many, many Ted Bains looking up at me from the floor. In the kitchen, all the cabinets had been opened and what cookware there was pulled onto the floor. In the middle of that mess was a green button down shirt that said Bennigan's over the heart.

Adding it all up, Ted Bain was a wannabe actor/model who worked as a waiter. An American cliché. Someone who normally wouldn't be that interesting. Except now he was. He was a fugitive, and they were always interesting.

15

"Louis, you had me to dinner yesterday," I said into the receiver. I'd barely walked in when the phone rang. It was around six-thirty.

"Are you inviting us up, then?"

"God no," I said, quickly. There was nothing in my refrigerator except a half a dozen Budget Gourmets. Something I imagine he already knew since he'd poked around my kitchen at breakfast.

"Come down whenever you're ready," he said and hung up.

I had planned to curl up on my sofa, eat one of the Budget Gourmets—I was partial to the Swedish meatballs—and watch a couple of movies I'd brought home from Pinx: *Coal Miner's Daughter* and *All That Jazz*. But since I'd learned several things about Guy Peterson's murder since breakfast, I felt I owed it to Marc and Louis. I'd try to be back upstairs by eight so I could watch at least one of the movies.

I changed into an old baggy sweater—that, sadly, looked like something Bill Cosby might wear—and a pair of comfy shorts, and went downstairs barefoot. When I got to the courtyard, I saw the table was set for four with a lit candelabra in the center.

Leon came out of the apartment with a Mexican beer in his hand saying, "We're having *cerveza*."

Louis was right behind him carrying a basket of chips and a bowl of salsa. "I made an enchilada casserole. It's a weeknight so nothing fancy."

"Louis was just catching me up," Leon said. "Finding a corpse, you are a busy boy."

"He's been ruthlessly interrogated by the police," Louis said. "Don't leave that out."

"Twice," I said, though neither time was exactly ruthless.

"Really?"

"Yeah, Detective O'Shea stopped by Pinx this morning."

"What did Tall, Dark and Menacing want?" Louis asked.

"He wants to find Ted Bain."

"Does that mean they don't think you killed Guy the Camera Guy?"

"I think it means something else. I think they want something he has or something he knows. Something that has to do with Guy's death."

"And Mr. Crispy's, too," Leon said.

"Detective Thomas Gaines," Louis said.

"We think," I corrected.

"Can I get you a beer?"

"Um, I'm not big on beer," I explained. It made me feel too full. "Do you have any wine?"

"Red or white?"

"What goes with an enchilada casserole? I always forget," Leon interrupted before I could answer.

"It's a chicken casserole," Louis said.

"Ah, white then."

"Yes, I'll have white, thanks."

Leon and I sat down. He took a chip and dipped it into the bowl of salsa. "So, I missed the memorial service for the man who wasn't dead yet. What is his family going to think having to bury him twice?"

"They hadn't released the body, so they didn't bury anyone. I doubt they've released the real Guy either."

"I'm piecing this together. Someone died in the fire, possibly this Detective Gaines. Guy Peterson disappeared so he must have had something to do with that. Someone shot Guy. Presumably, that someone also had something to do with Gaines' death. Then, Guy's body was dumped behind your store, which means that you now have something to do with all of this."

I thought about what he'd just said. It was all true and yet it didn't feel especially true. It left out a lot. I decided to give it a shot myself.

"Things began before the riots. Guy did a photo shoot and managed to get an exhibit at a gallery. When the gallery owner started doing publicity she was threatened. Something about the photos made the police want to shut her down. But they haven't tried to come and get the photos from me even though they know I have them. Ted Bain has gone into hiding and the police are desperate to find him."

"Interesting," Leon said. "Your double murder doesn't sound very much like mine."

"Yet," I said. "We're still missing big parts of the story."

Louis came back and set a glass of white wine in front of me. I took a sip; it was very tart.

"So, what did you find out today, Noah?"

"How do you know I found out anything? I do have a business to run, you know."

Louis sat down and stared at me. "I'm waiting."

"I went to the gallery and talked to the owner. She said some weird things about Guy's photographs and I left. I stopped off and asked Guy's father why he'd identified the wrong body and he said the LAPD pushed him into that. I found out where Ted Bain lived and went—"

"I think I hear Marc," Louis said. "We should wait for him." He got up and went to get a beer. He was right; there was the sound of footsteps on the stairs and moments later Marc appeared in the courtyard. He came right over to the table and peeled off his jacket. He took a pack of cigarettes out of his shirt pocket saying, "Oh my God, what a day. They actually expected me to do something." He worked in the art department for television distribution repackaging old sitcoms and new talk shows for syndication.

Lighting a cigarette as he talked, he continued, "I had a two-hour meeting about the color red. It was for this new talk show. I don't know what this girl was in before, but she lost a hundred pounds and apparently that's enough to make you famous these days. Anyway, we started talking about Pantone colors and her eyes glazed over. I had to resort to fruit. Do you like strawberry red or apple red? What do you think of ketchup red? It was mind-numbing."

"Which red did she choose?" Louis asked, setting a beer in front of him.

"Radish."

"I never know what to make of a radish," Leon said. "Do people really eat them? Or is it just there in the supermarket to make the other vegetables look good?"

"People eat them," Louis said. "You can roast them. I'll make them sometime with a London Broil."

"I did get some time to work on our investigation," Marc said.

"Oh, don't call it that," I said, though I can't say exactly why. It was what we'd been doing, after all.

"There's no other word for it," Marc said.

"I just don't like the official sound of it."

"When I grow up I want to be Angela Lansbury," Leon said.

"You'd look good in a sweater set and pearls," Louis told him.

"Do you know that show's been on for eight years? That's more than a hundred and sixty dead bodies she's accidentally tripped over."

"Marc, what did you find out?" I asked, getting impatient with all the talk about *Murder, She Wrote*.

"Well, remember I thought there was some connection between the Trailblazers and the Frontier Scouts in Guy's pictures? I decided I should really find out more about the Trailblazers."

"How did you do that?" Louis asked.

"I dialed information. I thought I'd be lucky to get one number, but I was on with the operator for at least ten minutes. It's quite an organization. They have directors of this and managers of that and executive managers of other things. Finally, she found me a number for the executive director of the Trailblazer program, this guy named Wally George. So I called him."

"What was that like?" I prompted.

"I pretended I had a son who was a Frontier Scout and considering the Trailblazer program. So I had Wally tell me all about it. The kids work after school and weekends. In the summer they work a regular schedule—for which they're not paid by the way. They learn about law enforcement. That's what they're getting, supposedly. But then the conversation started to get weird."

"Wait a minute," Leon said. "Systematically breaking child labor laws wasn't weird enough?"

"It's worse than that. I have to pay fees for my son and buy him expensive uniforms."

"I told you I didn't want children," Louis said. "This is why."

"Shut up. So, the whole time Wally keeps bringing up the importance of family and family values, and making men out of these boys, *real* men. Finally he asks me 'what church I took my family to?' I'm at a complete loss. I haven't been to church in nearly a decade. I drew a blank. Finally, I said, 'Holy Virgin Mother of Christ.'"

"That's not a church," Louis pointed out.

"I know, right? But he says, 'Oh, Catholic' like I'd just mentioned I had foot fungus. I knew right then I'd made a mistake, so I did some quick thinking and told him it's my wife who's Catholic."

"And as a matter of fact, I am," Louis said.

"I tell him I'm really a Baptist, and imply that this has been a constant source of pain for me, bringing up my children Catholic. So then Wally starts to tell me that my son will get the right sort of religious instruction from the Trailblazers, that they'll make a man out of him, and that they have these retreats with the officers once a month."

"Well, that all sounds kind of pervy," Leon said.

"Don't say anything else important," Louis said. "I think the casserole is done."

He ran into the apartment.

"Well, don't you hate this weather?" Leon said. "I thought we were supposed to have June Gloom in June not May."

"This isn't June Gloom, it's May Gray," Marc said. "Obviously you're not a native."

"And neither are you. I don't think there is such a thing as a native Californian."

"I saw one once," I said. "In an exhibit at the L.A. zoo."

And then Louis was back with a glass baking dish full of bubbling, cheesy casserole. Marc moved the candelabra and Louis set the dish in the middle of the table.

"Louis, that looks wonderful," Marc said. I had the feeling he said that a lot.

As he dished out the casserole, Louis said, "I have something to contribute to the investigation." He paused dramatically and handed me a plate with far too much food on it. "After dinner, we'll be going on a field trip. So, eat up boys." He smirked as he dished out the casserole.

It was delicious. I ate nearly half my portion.

"Couldn't we have driven?" Leon asked, as we walked down the hill.

"It's two blocks."

"Yes, but two blocks downhill now is two blocks uphill later."

"Leon, behave or there will be no dessert for you," Louis said, under his arm was a manila envelope. To me he explained, "So, I took those two boxes of photos to work with me and locked them in a drawer."

"That was a good idea. Thanks."

"And then I went through them at lunchtime."

"You have photos in that envelope, don't you?" I said.

"Very good, Sherlock."

"And you think they're going to tell us something?"

"Let's not get ahead of ourselves," he said, as we turned into a small park, the name of which was on a sign at the gate, but that sign had been tagged so many times it was unreadable.

It was nearly seven, the sun was setting and it would be dark soon. I didn't like the idea of being in the park after dark. It was well lit, but that had never dampened its bad reputation. We passed a concrete picnic table. Four Latino teenagers in loose jeans, over-sized sweatshirts and tattoos were hanging out there.

"If you boys have a hankering for some crystal, now would be a good time," Leon teased.

"Have you ever tried crystal?" I asked him.

"Why, no, officer, I was just holding that for a friend."

I took that as a yes.

"What about you?" he asked me.

"I never did anything worse than cocaine and not a lot of that."

"Louis, where are you bringing us?" Marc asked.

"Just relax, we're almost there."

We were halfway through the park. We'd gone past the parking lot, the playground for tots and the picnic area with the tables and public grills. Abruptly, Louis stopped.

We stood in front of a tree. A distinctive tree, with a thick trunk and a tangled map of roots surrounding it. Its branches hung low and it was covered in newly emerged green leaves.

"It's a fig tree," Louis said.

"What does botany have to do with murder?" Leon asked. It was a good question, I had a feeling I knew why we were standing there, but I didn't know for sure until Louis took the photos out of the envelope.

Before he'd gotten them all the way out, I said, "Oh my God, the tree. It's in the pictures."

"Oh no," Marc said. "This is where that guy was killed."

"What guy?" I asked.

"You didn't live here yet," Louis said.

"It was two years ago, I think, when all those gay bashings were happening," Marc explained. "The guy's name was Pachuk —which I remember because it sounds like paycheck. I know, weird."

"Wait. What gay bashings?" I asked.

"Teenagers beating up guys every so often. The LAPD did nothing of course, except make it sound like gangs. There were even a couple of articles about tension between the gays and the Latinos in Silver Lake. Then this Pachuk guy died and the LAPD finally cracked down. But mostly on gay guys, arresting them for being drunk or in the wrong place." Marc took a photo from Louis.

Leon and I took a photo too. Standing there we studied them. The fig tree was behind the line of policemen. In some pictures you could barely see it at all; in others it was very prominent.

"Is anyone else thinking what I'm thinking?" Louis asked.

"I am," I said. It was starting to make sense. "When I went to the gallery this afternoon, the owner said the photos were true. I said, they're obviously staged and she agreed, but she still insisted that they were true."

"So, Guy the Camera Guy re-created something he'd seen before," Leon said. "He witnessed it."

"No, not Guy," I said. "If he was the witness he could have spoken up himself. The witness has to be Ted Bain. He's what Percy and O'Shea want. They don't want the pictures they want the witness."

16

THE NEXT MORNING, WHEN I LEFT TO GO TO PINX, I GOT to the bottom of the stairs and noticed there was an unmarked car blocking me in. I walked over and saw that Javier O'Shea was in the driver's seat. He was alone in the car.

"Are you afraid I'm going to make a run for it?"

"There's no parking on your street."

"Well, you're a public servant, do something about it."

I think he might have smiled a little at that, but I wasn't sure. I was exhausted and bleary-eyed, so I wasn't trusting what was in front of me. I'd stayed up late enough to watch both of the movies I'd brought home. Well, I sort of watched them. They were meant to take my mind off things, but I couldn't help thinking about what we thought we knew. That certain members of the LAPD had encouraged Trailblazers to beat up gay men, eventually resulting in the death of one of those men. It was the opposite of what those teenagers were supposed to be learning; they were supposed to be learning to uphold the law. Instead, they were learning how to break it.

Looking at O'Shea, I couldn't help but feel some revulsion. "Are you involved in the Trailblazer program?" I asked without thinking it through.

"What? Why are you asking about that?"

"A friend wants to send his kid," I lied. "Do you know anything about it?"

"No, I'm not involved with that. It's kind of exclusive."

"I imagine you're not white enough."

He was a little taken aback by my honesty, but he couldn't say I was wrong. "Yeah, something like that. I went to see the woman who owns that gallery. I showed her a picture of Gaines. It was Percy and Gaines who threatened her."

What was he up to? I wondered. He sounded like he suspected his partner of something, but I didn't believe it for a second. He just wanted me to think he was a good guy. There was no way—

"Unfortunately, she doesn't know specifically why she was threatened or, if she does, she isn't saying."

It sounded like she hadn't told him the pictures were 'real.' She must not have trusted him any more than I did.

"And I went by to see the Petersons at the Mondrian.

"The Mondrian Hotel? Isn't that a little pricey?"

"They think the LAPD is going to pay for it. They hired a lawyer and they're trying to sue us for telling them their son was dead when he wasn't."

"But Mr. Peterson identified the body."

"Yeah, now he's saying he never identified the body. That it was all Percy. That he just said what Percy wanted him to say."

"You don't believe that, do you?"

"I don't believe he misses his son, beyond that I'm not sure what I believe." He gave me a hard look and asked, "Are you ready to tell me where Ted Bain is?"

"I don't know where he is," I said. Surprisingly, that was true.

"Percy is looking for him. If he matters to you at all you'd better hope I find him first."

He held out a business card. I took it and looked at it, but it didn't make much sense.

"What is this?"

"It's someone in Internal Affairs. Give it to Ted Bain and tell him he can trust that person. And if he won't trust them, call information and contact the FBI."

Then he drove away. I was left standing there wondering, *who was that?* I'd been fairly certain all along that O'Shea was one of the bad guys. Now I wasn't so sure. I mean, it seemed like he was doing a good thing. But I still couldn't help wondering if it was a trick of some kind. I wondered, too, if this meant he wasn't going to be following me around anymore? That would be nice.

When I got to Pinx, Missy had already opened. It was Mikey's day off. I tried to stay around the store a bit more on Mikey's days off just in case. I didn't think anything would go wrong, but he made a point of suggesting I be there so if something did go wrong I'd never hear the end of it.

"I'm sorry about your friend Lainey," I told Missy once I got behind the counter with her.

She gave me a funny look. "She quit. She didn't die. I mean, we're still friends."

"Okay, well, if you have any other friends who might like to work here."

"Lainey."

"But she quit."

"She's willing to come back for a quarter more an hour."

"Why does she want a quarter more an hour?"

"Hazard pay."

I knew I was a soft touch but this was ridiculous. "If Lainey wants her job back she just needs to call me, but, no, she's not getting a raise."

Missy frowned. I was sure her next move was to get an even bigger raise for herself. The words "but I've been here longer than Lainey, I deserve fifty cents more an hour" hung in the air.

"And do me a favor. Don't giggle when people rent porn."

"The titles are funny."

"Just don't."

I excused myself and went back to the office where I called Ivy Bell. Her answering machine picked up. I almost left a message but hung up. Thinking about Ted's apartment stopped me. If that same someone broke into Ivy's, they'd know I was looking for Ted. I was pretty sure Percy already knew I was looking for Ted, and certainly O'Shea knew. Maybe it didn't matter.

Deciding to leave a message, I called again. This time the phone was picked up right away. I had the feeling I might have accidentally stumbled onto some code of sorts. Call twice, and I'll pick up the second time.

"Ivy?" I asked.

"Yeah? Who's this?"

"This is Noah Valentine at Pinx Video."

"Oh God. Ted told me you were sticking your nose into things."

Well, at least I wouldn't have to explain much.

"I'm trying to reach Ted. Could you tell him I have a phone number for someone at Internal Affairs? Someone who can keep him safe."

"Um, yeah I could tell him that. If I hear from him."

Then she hung up on me so hard I pulled my ear away from the phone.

I spent a little bit of time working on the tax stuff, but it was deadly boring so I went out to the front. Missy was hanging on the phone, something that I discouraged when there were customers in the store, and since there were two women in the store I gave Missy a look. She said, "Gotta go" into the phone. Putting the receiver back in the cradle, she said, "Lainey will be in on Friday."

"Good."

We sat there quietly for a moment and then I said, "Why don't you pick out a movie to put in, something that hasn't been going out a lot." It actually did work. People would rent movies right out of our VCR.

She'd only been gone a moment when a middle-aged woman with salt-and-pepper hair came up to the counter and laid out three gay porn videos in front of me. *A View to a Thrill*, *Man of the Year* and *Idol Eyes*. My first thought was that she was some sort of Christian who was now going to scold me. Instead, she looked up at me and asked, "How do you choose?"

"I'm sorry?"

"How do you decide which one you want to see?"

"Um, well," I was turning really red. "It depends on which of the models you like best."

"But, is there a story? They just have the actors' names on the back so it's hard to tell."

I pointed to *A View to a Thrill* and said, "This is sort of James Bond take-off." Oh God, I was making a double entendre. Missy came back and picked up the gist of the conversation.

"You really shouldn't pay too much attention to the story. They certainly didn't." I cleared my throat. "These are all really good choices, though. Very popular."

The woman continued to ruminate.

Missy said, "I picked out *Breakfast at Tiffany's*, but if you'd rather play one of those…"

"Very funny."

"I'll take this one," the woman said, pointing at *Idol Eyes*. Handing me her membership card she said, "I think he has kind eyes."

"You know, a lot of people mention that," I lied.

The phone rang as I checked the woman out. Missy answered, saying brightly, "Pinx Video."

"Uh-huh, who's calling?" She listened. "Well, why don't you want to tell me?"

That set off alarm bells. "Is that for me?" I asked as I ripped the woman's receipt out of the printer. She just needed to sign it so I could rip off the tabs and give her the yellow copy. Luckily, she was going to pay on return.

"He doesn't want to say who it is," Missy said, clearly annoyed.

"That's okay. Tell him to hold on."

The woman, whose name was Ann Choad, took an inordinate time with her signature. Most people simply scrawled something at the bottom of the form, but Ann Choad was taking care with each letter. I raised my eyebrows at Missy and switched places with her.

"Hello?"

"This is Ted. Meet me on the trail up by the Griffith Observatory. The East Trail. Don't let anyone follow you."

And then he hung up.

Missy stared at me. "That was a quick call."

"I have to go."

"But what if something happens?"

"You'll be fine, really."

"Should I call Mikey?"

"No. Do not call Mikey. I'll be back in an hour. You'll be fine."

And she would be fine. I hoped.

I gathered my things and walked out back to my car. As I did, I thought, *Make sure no one follows me.* That just sounded ridiculous. What had happened to my life? Buildings were burning, bodies were showing up, I was investigated, threatened, and now I had to worry about being followed. How had this happened to me?

I got into my car and started it. Looking around I tried to see if any of the cars in the parking lot had a driver. None did. I backed up and took the exit ramp up to the street.

Watching traffic, I turned north on Hyperion. I scanned the cars behind me. I couldn't believe it when a gray sedan pulled away from the curb so quickly it nearly got hit by a little Jeep. The sedan, which was about the size of a bedroom, stayed in the lane behind me.

Continuing down Hyperion, I wondered what to do. I didn't know how to lose a tail. I mean, I'd seen it a million times on TV, but how did you really do it? At Griffith Park Boulevard, I pulled over into the left turn lane without signaling. The light turned yellow, then red. I didn't have the nerve to speed through. I just sat there, waiting, with the gray sedan sitting two cars behind me.

When I had the light, I made a left-hand turn and then, at the last possible moment, made a sudden right turn into the

Mayfair's parking lot. I saw the sedan continue on, unable to make the turn in time. I drove around the parking lot as though I was looking for a spot, keeping an eye on the entrance. And then, on my second turn around the lot, the sedan pulled in. I immediately pulled out of the parking lot onto Griffith Park Boulevard.

I sped down to the next intersection and turned right. The sedan had not appeared in my rear view mirror. I passed Marshall High, turning onto Franklin right before the Shakespeare Bridge. The only car behind me was a small blue sports car, I was fairly sure of that. Still, I raced along the streets at about fifty miles an hour, far too fast for residential streets and far too fast for my little car.

I turned north on Hillhurst, losing myself in the traffic. I was fine. I was sure of it. I did wish I hadn't bought a red car. I'm sure there were better colors for when you were attempting to lose a tail. Gray, for instance.

Crossing Los Feliz, I followed the signs for the Observatory and in a few minutes I was in Griffith Park, passing the Greek, rising into the hills, the terrain around me becoming scraggly and ragged.

Five minutes later, I was at the Observatory and parking alongside the road. I got out of the car and walked toward the famous building. I couldn't help it; I had to turn around to see if I was being followed. There were a lot of cars but no gray sedan anywhere in sight.

I scanned the grounds looking for the trail. I really had no idea where it began. Was it even on this side of the street? I was nearly to the steps when I noticed a dirt path to the left. *That must be it,* I thought. How was I going to find Ted Bain? Was he somewhere nearby watching for me? Checking to see that I wasn't being followed?

I followed the trail down below the Observatory. Fortunately, it was a cool day thanks to more May Gray. I had on a thick polo shirt, jeans and a pair of Reeboks. I didn't expect to break a sweat. The trail descended down the hill at a steep enough slope that it increased your speed noticeably as you walked down. Soon I came upon a juncture where I could turn either east or west. At the juncture was a bench pointed at an amazing view of L.A. Ted Bain sat on that bench taking in the view.

I sat down next to him and looked over. The trail was dusty. Some of the dust covered his face, and so had the tears he'd been crying. Together they'd made a few muddy streaks across his cheeks.

"I'm sorry about Guy," I said.

He shrugged like it didn't matter. I knew that it did.

"You've found some place safe?"

"Yes."

I didn't ask where. "I have this card for you. It's Internal Affairs at the LAPD. I think if you contact them they will be able to help you. If you don't trust them, you can call the FBI."

He nodded. Emotion seemed to overwhelm him. It must be pretty terrifying to need the services of the FBI.

"I think I understand what happened," I said. "You saw the police kill someone and now they want to kill you."

"Not the police. The Frontier Scouts." He was silent for a moment. "I, um, I went to the park. I used to party sometimes. I had a couple of days off and I had the urge. I went down to the park to score, but the, uh, dealers weren't there. I walked deeper in, looking for them. That's when I saw what those kids were doing. The policemen were encouraging them, yelling at them to…"

He swallowed hard.

"I ran home. I don't think they knew. I don't think they saw me. I knew I couldn't tell anyone. I mean, they were wearing uniforms, you know? It wasn't hard to figure out who they were. So, I kept my mouth shut."

"Until Guy came up with a plan to help you?"

"Help me? I wouldn't say that's the right way to look at it. Help me." He gave me an ironic smile. "I met Guy, we started hanging out. I wasn't ever going to tell anybody what I saw, but I had these dreams. Dreams about what I'd seen. One night I told him."

"And that's when he took the photos."

"I didn't know he was going to do that. I would have tried to stop him. I didn't want—"

"Why did he do it then?"

"Money."

"He wanted to blackmail the police?"

"He didn't tell me that. He told me he took the pictures to keep me safe. And when he'd tell me that, it made sense. But then later, when I thought about it… It didn't make sense, you know?"

"So, the night the camera shop burned. He went there to meet Detective Gaines. To blackmail him."

Ted nodded. "He got the exhibit. There were a couple of pictures in the press before it opened. And the police showed. Just like he thought they would."

"The night the store burned, that wasn't the first time he'd met Gaines?"

"No. They'd talked before." He stopped, looked a bit confused then went on, "Guy wanted to move to New York, Manhattan. That's where the real photographers are. He said he wanted to take me with him."

"Why did he think he'd get money from cops? They don't make that much."

"Good cops don't make that much. But these weren't good cops."

"Did Guy kill Gaines?"

Ted shrugged. "He must have. He came to my place with blood on his clothes. He wouldn't talk about it, though. He said that would just make things worse. It must have been self-defense. Gaines must have tried to kill him first. Because, well, there was no money in killing Gaines so why would he have done it?"

"And you still planned to go to New York with him even after…"

"I loved him. I still do."

"When was the last time you saw him?"

"Saturday night. He said he was going to get money. He

said I should pack. So I did. I packed. And then I waited. He never came back."

"What money, though?" I asked. "Gaines didn't pay, did he?"

"I don't think this was the first time he'd blackmailed some-one. He said he had a benefactor, that's how he got the camera shop. I don't think he made much money from it, yet he always had cash. Just…never enough."

There was a movement behind us and I turned to see Nino Percy holding a handgun in both hands. It was aimed at Ted.

"Don't move," he said. "Don't you fucking move."

Oh my God, I thought. *I've led the police right to Ted.* They'd probably kill him. And it was my fault.

17

—————

I heard the helicopter before I understood why it was there. It hovered close overhead, as I realized it was there for us. Then, a half a dozen police officers came down the slope. They wore windbreakers that said LAPD on the back and held handguns in front of them.

O'Shea had set me up. He'd used me to flush Ted out. I felt terrible. I'd betrayed poor Ted without even knowing it. Was he going to be found dead in a couple of days down at County Jail? Would he conveniently "hang himself" in his cell before the end of the week?

It took the stoic dead look on Percy's face before I realized I was wrong, they weren't there for us. They were there for Percy.

Officers began to call for Percy to drop his weapon. He wasn't doing it, though. I touched Ted on the arm and then slowly took a step backward. If there was going to be shooting I didn't want to be anywhere near it.

But then, Percy dropped his gun and was immediately swamped by blue windbreakers. Moments later he was in cuffs being led up the trail. Ted and I stood there not knowing what to do. He was shaking again. I wondered if he was going into shock.

And then Detective O'Shea was standing next to us. He'd

been hard to pick out because he wore the same dark blue wind-breaker everyone else wore.

I didn't wait for him to speak. "You tricked me. You only gave me that information so you could follow me to Ted."

O'Shea ignored me. "You're Ted Bain?"

Ted nodded his head.

"Are you all right? You look a little bit shaky."

Ted took a few deep breaths and then said, "Is this over? Is this really over?"

"You're going to be fine. Just breathe."

He glanced at me. I tried to burn a hole in his face with my eyes. It didn't work.

"I'd like you both to come back to Rampart and make a statement."

"How do we know we'll be safe?"

"We just arrested an officer with fifteen years under his belt right in front of you. I think that should count for something."

That was actually true. If they were just trying to get to Ted to kill him, they'd put on a very elaborate show.

O'Shea led us up the trail. When we got to the lawn we saw that the area was filled with cops. Down at the turnaround in front of the Observatory was a parking lot full of squad cars, with O'Shea's gray sedan in the middle of them. When we got to the car, O'Shea opened the back door for us. Ted slid in.

Before I got in, I said, "You were following me."

"And I lost you."

"Then, how did you…"

"We were following Percy, too. He was behind you in a blue Toyota MR2."

"What is that?"

"It's a mid-engine sports car." He held my eyes for a second. "Look, neither of you were ever in any real danger."

"Yeah, that's what it felt like when Percy held a gun on us."

There wasn't a lot O'Shea could say to that, so I got into the car. He closed the door, then worked on getting a couple of black-and-whites moved so we could get out.

"Is it really over?" Ted asked, in a very small voice.

"Yes, it is."

"I asked that already, didn't I?"

"It's okay. There's a lot to take in."

O'Shea got in the car and we took off.

Rampart Station is a rectangular brick box inside a spider-like stucco frame on Benton Way a few blocks from my apartment. O'Shea parked illegally in front of the building and we got out. Then we were led up a short flight of stairs into the building.

Inside, we walked down a narrow hallway and eventually we were each put into a different interrogation room. Mine was small, windowless and stuffy. After a few minutes, a uniformed officer came in and gave me a legal pad and a pen.

"Detective O'Shea requests that you write down whatever you can think of related to today's events."

Then he left.

When it came right down to it, there wasn't much for me to write. I got a phone call from Ted asking me to meet him on the trail at the Observatory. I met him at the appointed spot and we talked for maybe ten minutes. Then, Detective Percy approached us holding a gun. The gun was aimed at us. Then the cavalry arrived. It was a pretty short statement.

After about a half an hour, O'Shea came in to talk to me.

"Did you finish with Ted?" I asked.

"No. We're taking a break, though. He's been through the ringer." He pulled my statement toward him and read it.

"Succinct," he said when he finished.

"I didn't see any point in going on and on." Then I asked, "When did you know Percy was bad?"

"I see you're still asking the questions," he said, but there was a smile on his face when he said it. "I began to suspect Nino when you started saying things that didn't make sense."

I nodded.

"So, today? You got a call from Ted out of the blue?"

"No. I called his friend Ivy and left a message for him with her. About the information you gave me."

"Good."

"So, Detective Percy killed Guy Peterson?" I asked.

"It's early in the process. He's requested a lawyer, so it will be difficult to get information for some time."

Something wasn't sitting right with me, but I couldn't quite put my finger on exactly what. "He's not going to get away with it, is he?"

"At this point, I think we have a better case in the Pachuk murder. I just took Ted Bain's statement on that. While Percy did not take part directly in the killing, the relationship between the detective and the Trailblazers will likely mean he'll be charged."

"Once you establish which boys were there, do you think it will be easy to get a least one of them to implicate him?"

"I probably shouldn't comment on that…" he said, but he gave me a wink that answered my questions. And I was glad. Part of me hoped they threw the book at the adults and let the kids off lightly. I wasn't sure the kids would have done anything if not for the encouragement of men like Percy and Gaines.

"I'm sorry," I said abruptly.

"What are you sorry about?"

"I thought you were in on things with Percy. I thought you were a bad guy."

"Yeah, that came across. It's fine, though. I can't blame people for not trusting the LAPD. A lot of bad things have happened and it will take time for us to rebuild trust with the community."

"Do you think you ever will?" I asked.

"Of course. It's our job."

O'Shea had a uniform drive me back to my car in Griffith Park. I didn't say a word to the driver the whole way. He didn't seem to mind.

It was almost six o'clock. I'd done a lot of waiting at Rampart and a lot of thinking. I should never have gotten involved with this. But if I hadn't, would Ted Bain be safe? Or for that matter would Guy Peterson be dead? How much had I changed things and what was I truly responsible for?

I should be happier, I thought. The people who deserved to be punished would be, or they were already dead. Gaines was complicit in the Pachuk murder, so you could say he got what he deserved. Percy deserved to be in prison and Guy, well, apparently he was a habitual blackmailer. Even if he killed Gaines in self-defense he was still a criminal. He may not have deserved to die, but that was a sentence Percy passed on him, not me.

I put my car into the carport and closed the metal gate. Walking up the stairs from the street I felt bone tired, like I could barely stand a minute longer. I wanted ice cream and an old movie. And sleep. I felt like I could sleep for a week.

As soon as I reached the courtyard I knew none of that was going to happen. There were nine people standing around, drinks in hand, nibbling at appetizers from a fancy spread on the table. A bouquet of balloons was tied to the birds of paradise. Marc yelled, "There he is!"

They started moving toward me. I almost ran. I only knew six of them: Marc and Louis, Leon, Deborah and Ron, and Jamie. The others were complete strangers.

"We saw you on the news," Louis said, slipping a glass of wine into my hand.

"They interrupted programming."

"I was in the middle of *One Life to Live,*" Jamie said.

"Noah, this is Pearl," Louis said, introducing me to a pretty black woman with caramel colored skin. "Pearl got us that information on Guy's landlord."

"Oh, right, thanks for that." It had made no difference, but still, it was nice of her. I leaned close to Louis and asked under my breath, "Who are these other people?"

"The tall guy is Casey Dillard. Picture him in a uniform."

"Oh, from the Gauntlet?"

"Yeah, we got friendly after you left."

"Oh, okay. And the blond?" There was a very attractive blond boy munching on chips and dip.

"Jamie brought a date."

Deborah pushed through. "What was it like, being held hostage at gunpoint?"

I think my eyes got kind of big. "I wouldn't describe it like that exactly…"

"That's what it looked like on TV."

I was confused. "No, it all happened really fast. It wasn't filmed, was it? I mean there was a helicopter. I thought it was a police helicopter."

"Oh my God," Jamie said. "The sky was full of helicopters. One station couldn't get close enough, so they started reporting on the helicopters reporting the stand-off."

"It wasn't a stand-off. The whole thing happened very quickly."

Didn't it? Or had I gone into some kind of shock and lost track of time?

"So, is this Percy guy Detective Tall, Dark and Menacing? Or is he the other one?" Marc asked.

"He's the other one."

"Thank God. It's a terrible when attractive people go bad."

"We were right all along," Leon said. "We knew the police were behind the whole thing."

"Well, not all of the police, just a couple really," I pointed out.

"How did all that happen?" Louis asked. "Last we knew you were still trying to find Ted Bain."

"Detective O'Shea gave me the card of someone to contact in Internal Affairs and told me to get it to Ted, and so I made a phone call and he called me back."

"O'Shea, that's Tall, Dark and Menacing?" Marc asked.

"Yes."

"And he's a good guy?"

"Yes. I think so."

"So then what happened?" the blond stranger asked me.

"Ted wanted me to meet him on one of the trails at the Observatory."

"Oh Jamie, we need to take you hiking up there. It's really

great," Deborah said.

"And you were followed?" Jamie's date prodded me.

"Yes, but they were following Percy, too."

"Oh, so they suspected him already."

"O'Shea did, yes."

"Actually, it's incredibly hard to tail someone in Los Angeles. You practically need a whole SWAT team to do it," Leon said.

"And how do you know that?" Louis wanted to know.

"I had a thing with one of the PAs on *Detective Dan*."

"*Detective Dan*? When was that on?"

"It wasn't. It was a pilot that didn't get picked up. But my PA did a lot of research."

"Jeez Leon, can't you screw somebody on a show that gets picked up?" Marc asked.

"I try."

Finally, I took a seat and refused to move. Louis brought me a plate of appetizers that looked wonderful and completely unappetizing at the same time.

"So, Louis," I asked, beginning to feel the wine. "That tree in the park. How did you even know about it?"

"Actually, it's a well known cruising area and, well, I was a more adventurous person before I met Marc." He sat down with me and for a moment let the party run itself. "How does it feel?"

"I'm not sure yet."

"Because of us—well, mainly you—the people responsible for a string of gay bashings and a gay man's death will be punished. I think that's pretty cool."

"Because of Ted Bain and Guy Peterson."

"Well, no, from what you've said, Ted Bain was never going to say a word and Guy Peterson only wanted to profit from the information. You're not comfortable playing the hero, are you?"

"I'm hardly a hero."

"You didn't have to do any of the things you did. You could have stayed in hiding."

"I'm not in—" I began to say, but I couldn't even raise the energy to argue.

18

WHEN I WOKE THE NEXT MORNING, I REALIZED THAT something had been gnawing at me. Percy would not have killed Guy, not without knowing where Ted Bain was. And then there was the money. Guy had gone to get the money. So where was it? And did it even exist?

Guy was going to get money. Did that mean he already had the money and had hidden it? Or was he going to blackmail someone? And if he was, who was that someone...

I made myself a pot of coffee—I didn't think it was so horrible to buy your coffee already ground, I certainly couldn't tell the difference—and poured myself a bowl of Barbara's organic corn flakes with enough sugar to erase any and all health benefits of the cereal. I'd only had a few bites when I had an idea.

I went and got my phone off its base. Dialed a number out of my address book and waited.

"This is Leon Arlo."

"Leon, this is Noah."

"Oh hello. What are we going to solve now, the Lindbergh kidnapping or the Black Dahlia?"

"Can you get me on the lot? I want to see Rex Hoffman again."

"Oh? Have you decided to take him up on his very generous offer?"

"No. I want to see if Guy came back and tried to blackmail him again."

"Why does that matter?"

"I'm not sure it does. But I'd like to know."

"All right. I'll get a drive-on for you. When do you want it for?"

"In about half an hour."

"All right. Meet me in front of the Zukor building."

"You want to go with me?"

"I'm not going to let you have all the glory."

I wasn't sure glory was the only thing he was after.

After a quick shower, I dressed in a pair of beige 501s, my oxblood Docs and a navy blue work shirt. My hair was hopeless, so I put on a baseball cap emblazoned with the logo for the failed talk show, *Minty*, that Marc had given me. He had fifty in a box under the bed. I was out the door in fifteen minutes and at the studio gates ten minutes after that.

I gave my name to the guard, a different guard this time, and when he had trouble finding it, I said, "Try Nora Balentine."

"Oh yeah. That some sort of joke?"

"Supposedly."

He chuckled and let me onto the lot. I parked and walked down to the Zukor building, a five-story gray-and-white layered cube. Leon stood in front of the entrance wearing a double-breasted gray suit and a daringly lavender tie.

"Good morning," Leon said. "Welcome to the coal mines. This is where the magic happens in unmagical ways."

We walked by a couple of soundstages and then turned to the left. I remembered the way, but I didn't need to. Leon was very familiar with the lot.

"Do you know what you want to say to him?" Leon asked as we stood before the entrance to Stage 11.

"I think so."

"Good. We may not get much time. Follow my lead."

We walked into the soundstage and got about twenty feet before we were stopped by a guard.

"I don't think you're supposed to be in here."

I could see the stage for Hoffman's show on the other side of the stage. In daylight, it was garish oranges and reds, with light bulbs in those and other colors. Rex Hoffman stood in the center of the stage.

"We're friends of Mr. Hoffman's," Leon said confidently. "Can you tell him we're here?"

"Name?"

"Peterson. Guy Peterson."

The guard turned and walked away. I gave Leon a sidelong glance. "That was impressive."

"People are always curious when the dead show up for a chat."

It didn't take long before Rex Hoffman was standing in front of us.

"Hi. I'm Leon Arlo. Director, International Rights. Huge fan. Now, if there's anything I can—"

Hoffman ignored him, asking me, "What are you doing here?"

"I have a couple more questions I'd like to ask."

"Yeah, just because you were friends with Guy doesn't give you the right to show up here any time you want."

"You lied to me. You said you didn't pay Guy. I think that's wrong. I think you paid him."

"And why do you think that?"

"Because Guy's boyfriend said he went to get money the night he died. So either you gave him money or he came back to ask you again on the night he was killed."

"What are you—" I could see headlines flashing through his mind. He could probably get through some old sex pictures, but murder? "Yes. Of course, I paid him. The first time. I'm surprised you believed me."

"You didn't see him the night he died?"

"Of course not. Do you want me to provide an alibi? I think I remember his name."

I believed him, though, so I didn't ask.

"You gave Guy cash?" I asked.

"Of course, I gave him cash. Blackmailers don't take checks."

"I wouldn't know. I've never been blackmailed."

"Is that all? I'm in the middle of shooting a show. They can't do anything without me."

"Are you the only one?"

"Yes, I'm the only host—"

"No. Are you the only one Guy was blackmailing?"

He thought for a moment. "Probably not. He liked taking that kind of picture. He liked attractive men. It wouldn't surprise me if someone else fell into his trap. Now, if you'll excuse me."

"It was a pleasure meeting you," Leon said, extending his hand. Hoffman looked at it and then walked away. "I gather he was a lot friendlier the first time you saw him."

So where was the money? The most logical place to keep cash was in a safety deposit box. But I was pretty certain that Ted said Guy left at night to get the money, so that left out anything to do with a bank. That left his apartment and his store as the most logical places. Of course, his store had already burned, so it wasn't likely he kept the money there. That left his apartment.

After I left the studio, I took Western north. Guy's family had cleaned out his apartment. Did that mean they found the money? That would explain the Mondrian Hotel. But then, so would the settlement they're likely to receive from the insurance on Guy's store. Or even the settlement they were trying to squeeze out of the LAPD.

As I drove, I tried to calculate how much insurance might pay for his inventory. When I took his class he had maybe forty cameras, many of them quite expensive. And lenses, a lot of lenses. Then there were the furnishings and cash register, not worth much, and the equipment in the dark room. So, maybe twenty or thirty thousand dollars.

Of course, there would be a deductible and they wouldn't have paid this quickly. Not to mention, they'd probably never pay. It was likely Guy burned the place down himself. Insurance companies frowned on that.

Did that mean for sure his family found the money? Or was I just being a snob? They didn't seem like people who had much money, but maybe I was wrong. Maybe they had lots of money.

I turned around the lazy corner that meant Western was now Los Feliz. It was unlikely I'd find anything at Guy's apartment, I knew that. Hell, it was unlikely I'd even be able to get in. I tried to think of a story I could tell the manager if I needed to. That is, if there was a manager. There might just be a management company. In which case, I'd need a really good story.

I found a legal parking place on a side street and walked up to the building. I could call the management company and tell them I'd heard about the apartment and I wanted to see it. Could I get them to show it to me that afternoon? Probably. Money was involved.

I walked into the courtyard and climbed up to the second floor. There was no reason not to check and see if the Petersons hadn't simply left the door open. In a building like this there was really no reason not to leave an empty apartment open. I pulled open the screen door and tried the door to the apartment. Locked.

Taking a step back, I considered knocking on the neighbors' doors. Sometimes people left keys with a neighbor; Guy might have done that. While I was deciding between knocking on the door of 2E or 2G, I noticed Guy's window was open. I lifted the screen off and was able to step into the apartment through the window, which was exactly how he'd gotten into my apartment only a few nights before.

The apartment looked to be completely empty and smelled heavily of bleach. That might have been why the windows were open, but it wasn't doing much good. How much bleach had they used? And why? The wood floor would have only needed to be mopped with Murphy's Oil.

I stepped into the kitchen and saw that they'd barely cleaned the sink. Popping open the refrigerator, it was obvious they wiped it down with a sponge, but that was not the same as cleaning. The oven they'd ignored completely—despite the fact that it really needed it. A dirty oven didn't fit with someone who'd use so much bleach they had to leave a window open.

Pushing the thought out of my mind, I wondered where he might have hidden the money. Certainly it could have been in a piece of furniture no longer there, but I doubted Guy would put it anywhere as easy to find as under the mattress. It was thirty thousand dollars, after all. Or maybe even more than thirty.

I walked around the apartment looking in all the closets to see if there was a hatch into the attic. There wasn't. Then I went into the bathroom, lifted up the lid to the toilet, and looked into the tank. This might have been a good hiding place once, but it had been ruined by *The Godfather*. Now everyone knew the best place to hide a gun was in a Ziploc bag in the toilet tank. It would have worked for money, too. Running my hand around the underside of the sink, I found nothing.

I went back to the not-very-clean kitchen. The freezer was empty but for a bit too much frost. I checked the underside of each drawer. Then I opened the doors below the sink. That area was empty. I ran a hand around the underside of the kitchen sink. Part way through, I stopped. I'd come across something sticky. And there was something else, something still stuck to the underside of the sink.

It took a moment or two to dislodge it. When I pulled my hand back out from under the sink, I saw it was a piece of electrical tape. Something had been taped under the sink. Probably the money Ted had been talking about. Did that mean Guy gotten to it? Or did his family find it first? And if they did, what did he do when he found it wasn't there?

I was about to leave the apartment; I'd found what I needed to find, when I realized there was a large, funky looking spot on the wall next to the window. It was funky looking because the paint had been scrubbed off. The smell of bleach was very strong right there. I took a step back and tried to put it together. The scrubbed spot was taller than I was and twice as wide. As I stood staring at it, I realized something odd. Partway up, in the center were two spots that had been spackled.

Now, why would they spackle the walls but not clean the oven? I wondered. Not to mention the spots they spackled were too low for pictures. The hardwood floor was in decent shape, though hardly new. Most of the slats held their varnish, but the seal was old enough to have cracked between the slats. I got down on my knees. The floor beneath the scrubbed spot looked like it also had been washed in bleach. But there was something dark between the slats. I ran my thumbnail between two slats, pushing it in as deeply as I could.

When I took a closer look at my thumb, I recognized the sticky, dark material immediately. It was the same stuff I'd taken off the spanner wrench. It was dried blood. This whole area had been drenched in blood and then cleaned.

19

I WENT HOME AND DID THE SMART THING. I CALLED Rampart and asked for Detective O'Shea. He wasn't able to come to the phone. I left a message and asked that it be marked urgent. Then I waited.

It was after lunchtime so I made a tuna fish sandwich and ate half of it. There was nothing on TV except soap operas, and I didn't follow any of them. I could pick something out of my personal video collection, but I didn't have the patience. I felt an urgency about this. As though I knew if the Petersons left Los Angeles, they'd get away with Guy's murder.

I called the Mondrian and asked for their room. When the desk clerk put me through, I hung up. They were still there. Then I called back and asked about check-out time. Noon. Well, it was after noon so maybe they'd be staying another night. Or maybe they'd just be slipping away without checking out. People who committed murder didn't always follow the rules.

I waited almost an hour, then I called Rampart again and asked for Detective O'Shea. I was put on hold and had to wait. The phone was obviously being manned by a Trailblazer of probably sixteen or seventeen. It was a little creepy knowing what the boys had done, but then it probably wasn't this boy.

The beatings had all taken place two years ago. Those boys were off in college somewhere or had gone into the military. They definitely weren't answering the phones at Rampart now.

The boy came back and said, "Detective O'Shea is in the field. He's gotten your message and he'll call you as soon as he can."

"Can I leave another message?"

The boy sighed.

"Would you tell him that Guy Peterson's family killed him and that they might be leaving town."

"Okay," the boy said sounding a little bored. As though he got a similar message four times a day.

I didn't have anything to do with myself. I could have gone to Pinx and done some work, but I really couldn't focus on anything but mentally urging the phone to ring. Waiting for someone to call you is one of the worst things ever. Waiting for someone to call you regarding a murder is even worse.

I put *The Immaculate Collection* into the CD player and tried bouncing around the apartment to vintage Madonna just to shake off some energy. It didn't work. The energy just wouldn't be shaken off.

For the third time, I called Rampart Station. This time I knew I wouldn't get O'Shea on the phone. I left a message with one of the Trailblazers, "Please let Detective O'Shea know that I'm on my way to the Mondrian Hotel. I'll be in the lobby."

When I hung up, I stopped to think. I'd never been to the Mondrian before. I assumed there was a lobby. But it was unlikely they'd let me simply hang out there waiting to see if the Petersons tried to slink off. So, exactly what did I think I was going to do? It didn't take long before I had an idea. I went into my bedroom, pulled a suitcase out from under the bed, and began filling it with whatever I could grab.

The Mondrian was located in West Hollywood on the Sunset Strip, wedged between a couple of gigantic billboards—one selling a men's cologne by Halston and the other a new TV show about ESP. It was a twelve-story hotel that might have been kind of bland if they hadn't had an artist paint it up in every color of the rainbow. There were different blocks of color here and there, and it did have the feeling of an actual Mondrian.

I pulled up to the hotel and surrendered the Sentra to a valet. I could see that he was trying not to sneer at my car. I told him I was a guest checking in, got my suitcase out of the trunk, and slipped him a five. I tried to look like it had been an exhausting journey from Silver Lake. He gave me a ticket stub, took my keys, and didn't mention whether they'd validate at the front desk. My guess was they wouldn't.

I walked by a big teal-colored slab of marble, which said Le Mondrian Hotel in silver metal. That was the correct name of the hotel but everyone called it *The* instead of *Le*. There was no line at the front desk, so I carried my bag over and said to the clerk, "I'd like to book a room."

"Certainly, sir. Do you have a reservation?" She was a little too perky and her hair was caught in a nineteen-seventies time warp.

"No, this is a very spontaneous kind of trip."

She clicked away at a CRT. "Good news. We do have rooms available."

"Um, friends of mine are staying here. The Petersons. Could I be on the same floor with them?"

"Certainly, can you tell me what room they're in?"

"Oh gosh, you know they told me, but I'm kind of dyslexic. It might have been 651? Or maybe it was 868? You know, I'm sure there's a four in there somewhere."

She smiled at me. "Peterson, you said?"

"Yes."

"My sister is dyslexic. People treat her like she's stupid, and she's really not. Here we go. The Petersons are in room 723. I can put you in room 726. It's across the hall just kitty-corner to their room."

The three of them were sharing a room, apparently. I wondered if it was a suite. Then the clerk asked me for one hundred and seventy eight dollars and I understood why they were sharing a room. Even if I had thirty-thousand in cash I'd think that was a lot of money.

I gave the clerk my credit card, signed a small print agreement that gave them all the advantages, and received the key to my room. I declined her offer of a bellhop—I only had the one half-full bag, after all—and walked across the lobby to the elevators. I caught a glimpse of a bar sitting off the lobby and wondered if it might be a good place to keep a lookout.

When I reached the seventh floor I walked down the long hallway, hesitating at room 723. I listened. A television was playing, an action movie given the soundtrack, something recent off pay-per-view, probably. I continued to my room. If they were watching a movie, they weren't leaving anytime soon.

The room was nice, with a view of Sunset Boulevard and the hills behind the hotel. It would probably be very pretty once it got dark. There was a king-sized bed, a desk and an ultra-mod chair. Everything was done in white with splashes of primary colors to match the outside of the hotel.

I put my suitcase down and sat on the bed. Now what? I could call Detective O'Shea again to give him an update. Or rather, give the Trailblazer who answered the phone an update. I could sit in the room waiting. Or I could go down to the lobby bar and keep an eye out for O'Shea while making sure the Petersons didn't leave.

Before I left the room, I went into the bathroom to see what crazy thing my hair was doing. It was sticking up in the front and sloping off in a weird way on the right. I pushed it around until I thought it looked a little better, wishing I'd brought a hairbrush, and left.

The bar could be accessed from the lobby through a small arch. There were only a couple of stools that gave me a sight line to the main hotel entrance. The bar also gave a lovely view out to the pool on one side and a patio restaurant on the other.

There were a lot of out-of-towners by the pool. I knew they were from out of town because a high of seventy was considered downright chilly and most Angelenos considered it sweater weather. Only people used to temperatures below freezing considered it sunbathing weather.

I sat down on one of the stools that offered the sightline I wanted. The bartender was about my age, had his haircut into a bowl on top and shaved around the sides. I was pretty sure that was a popular cut with teen idols. He had a nice smile and friendly eyes. I ordered a Tanqueray martini straight up with a twist. I almost never had martinis, but it had seemed really elegant when Louis made one for Leon and this seemed the place to be elegant.

He made the martini quickly and charged me six dollars, which I thought was a lot. I asked him to charge it to my room. He lay the check down in front of me and pretended like he didn't care what happened to it.

"My name's Chuckie," he said.

"Noah."

"So, Noah, let me guess. You're in the entertainment business, right?"

"Um, yes. I am." I didn't really think about it that way, but I actually was in the entertainment business. People were entertained by the videos I rented them.

"Yeah, I'm good at that," he said. "Let's see, producer, writer, actor...director. My guess is you're a producer."

"In a way."

"Are you here for a meeting?"

"Sort of."

"With someone famous?"

"No." I decided I'd better make up a story if I wanted him to tell me anything about the Petersons. "There's a family staying here. From Fresno. Mother and father, daughter. There was a son but...he died in the riots. Practically ripped to pieces by the mob at..." Here I stumbled. All I could think of was Fredrick's of Hollywood and I couldn't say that he was ripped to pieces by a mob looting lingerie.

I didn't need to say anymore, though, because he said, "I think I saw that on TV."

"You probably did. Anyway," and here I lowered my voice,

though the bar was nearly empty. "I'm trying to buy the movie rights."

"Oh yeah, that would make a good movie."

"The mom and dad are in their late fifties early sixties. Gray. A little overweight. The daughter is mid-twenties, dark hair, a little—"

"Horsey?"

"Yes, that's her."

"She was in here last night trying to pick up guys."

"Really?"

"Yeah, eventually the father came down and they had a screaming match. He was trying to be reasonable at first, but she started screaming about how he never loved her, never even liked her. That he only ever liked…Gary?"

"Guy."

"That's right. Guy. He's the one who was…"

"Yes."

"Wow. She's kind of awful isn't she? I mean, the brother just died and she's doing a Smothers Brothers Mom-liked-you-best routine. You need another one of those, don't you?"

I looked down and realized I'd finished my martini. "Um, yeah, sure," I said. He started making the new drink. The thing with Cindy didn't surprise me much. There didn't seem to be much love lost between the siblings.

Chuckie finished making my drink and set the new one in front of me. "You might want to watch your step with those Petersons. When the dad dragged her out of here, that girl was yelling about faggots. You know, there might be some stuff going on with them that you don't want for your movie, if you know what I mean."

Unfortunately, I did.

20

I WAS A BIT TIPSY AFTER MY SECOND MARTINI. I DECIDED to go back up to my room and call my answering machine to see if I'd gotten a call from Detective O'Shea. And, if I hadn't, call him again.

Getting off on seven, I was part way down the hall when I heard the other elevator open and someone got out. Without thinking, I turned around and saw that the person getting out was Cindy Peterson. She had a big, fluffy hotel towel wrapped around her. Beneath was a black bathing suit. She had been at the pool while I was in the lobby bar.

I turned around quickly so she wouldn't get a good look at me. But it was too late. She had.

"What are you doing here?"

"I, uh, I, uh…won a contest for a free night."

"And you ended up on the same floor with me and my family? Yeah, that's bullshit. What are you really doing here?"

"I have to go," I said, and kept walking toward my room. Cindy grabbed a fist full of my hair and squeezed. "Oh, shit!"

I had a sudden flash of my dad. I was six or so and he was telling me to never hit a girl. That it was just wrong. Then he whispered in my ear so my mother couldn't hear him, "Never hit a girl because they don't fight fair."

As Cindy dragged me toward the Peterson's room, his point was driven home. I grabbed at her wrist trying to break her grasp on my hair, but she just would not let go. She did lose her towel, revealing the black one-piece she wore underneath. She smelled strongly of chlorine and coconut suntan oil. She must have left the oil at the pool though, since she wasn't carrying anything but the towel.

It didn't really take much to drag me over to Suite 723. The television was still playing. I could hear it as she pounded on the door. I tried to twist around so that I could kick her, but it didn't work. Honestly, it felt like she was pulling my hair out strand by strand. I wasn't happy about that. I mean, I'm not crazy about the things my hair does, but I do like it being on my head.

"What is this?" I heard her father ask when she opened the door.

"It's that asshole video guy who keeps showing up."

"What's he doing here?"

"Looking for us, Dad. What do you think he's doing here?"

"You think he's figured things out?"

"Did you figure things out?" She shook my head, causing intense pain. "Is that why you're here?"

I'd known I needed a haircut for weeks. Why hadn't I done anything about it? Things would have been harder for her if I'd had a decent trim. For that matter, I could have gotten a buzz cut. Maybe next time, I will.

"Yeah, that's why he's here," the mom said. She seemed a bit more confident than the last time I'd seen her.

"We should shoot him. Get the gun out of my suitcase."

"Oh no, we're not shooting him," Guy's mom said. "We couldn't get the body out of here without people noticing."

"And I'm not cleaning up a mess like that again," the dad said.

"Oh my God! You barely did anything," the mom said.

"It's not my fault I have a weak stomach."

"Well, we have to get rid of him somehow," Cindy said.

"Throw him off the balcony," the mom said. "It'll seem like he jumped."

"Not to be a spoilsport," I said. "But my room is across the hall. Are you going to say I broke in and committed suicide off your balcony?"

"They won't know you didn't go up to the roof."

"They will if it's locked up there."

I could feel them looking at one another, contemplating the risk involved.

"You could always take me up to the roof and throw me off," I suggested. "That way you'd know."

I wasn't really being a helpful murder victim, I just figured if they took me up to the roof there would be a half a dozen opportunities for me to escape. Not to mention we might run into people in the elevator or even on the roof. Witnesses to murder were always a buzz kill.

"We're going to have to chance it," Cindy said, dragging me across the room.

"Wait," the dad said. "This is getting out of hand."

"Getting out of hand?" the mom said. "You didn't think it was getting out of hand when your daughter shot your son and you decided it was a good idea to get rid of the body?"

"You decided. I just went along."

"This is a complete stranger. It should be easier to kill a complete stranger than it was to kill your own son."

"I didn't kill my own son. She did," he said. Even from my angle I could see that he was pointing at Cindy.

"Whatever, Dad," she said, and started pulling me toward the balcony.

She got me through the sliding glass door to the balcony and I got the brilliant idea to sweep my leg underneath her and knock her to the ground. Surprisingly, it worked.

Falling hard on her ass, she let go of my hair. I can't tell you how good that felt. I almost yelled, "Yippee." But then I realized I was trapped on the balcony, Cindy was blocking my way out and she was getting up. And then she launched at me, coming at me from below, pushing me up and over the wrought iron railing. I did a horribly frightening flip, reaching back and grabbing at two of the railing's iron rungs. I ended up hanging off the balcony, feeling just a little banged up.

Someone was screaming very loudly. Well, not someone, me. I didn't seem to be able to stop. Cindy hissed at me to shut up. I didn't.

Right below me was another balcony. There was only about four and a half or five feet between the bottom of the balcony I was hanging from and the railing for the balcony below me. I was able to get my feet onto that railing. It felt better, much better than my legs dangling in air. I stopped screaming. Kind of.

It wasn't a good situation, though. If I let go there was no guarantee I would fall forward onto the sixth floor balcony. I could just as easily fall backward and land in the restaurant outside the lobby bar seven floors below. Well, six and a half, but still. I knew I might have to take the chance, but I really didn't want to.

Then, just to make matters worse, Cindy began kicking at my hands with her bare feet. It hurt, but it just made me grab the railings harder. Then she was screaming, too.

"My toe, I stubbed my toe, fudge!"

That was so odd, I almost laughed. This girl who'd shot her brother and was well into the process of killing me couldn't say the word fuck.

I looked down. A small group of people was forming in the empty restaurant. It was nice to see them. It meant Cindy and her awful parents weren't going to get away with this. Everything was going to unravel for them. I wouldn't be here, but they'd pay for that. I had a moment of feeling strangely calm.

And then someone wearing a shoe kicked me. I heard Guy's mother say, "Goddamn it." My fingers were pretty close to the floor of the balcony and it was easy to miss.

But then, one of them was on their knees using their hands to pry my fingers away—

I heard a pounding at the door. "LAPD open up!"

I started screaming again—or maybe I'd never actually

stopped. But now there was someone to hear my screams, so I tried even harder. They pounded again, but no one inside the room moved. Someone, I'm not sure which woman, was still working at prying my fingers—

There was a loud thud and heavy footsteps and, presumably, the cops entered the room. I took a deep breath and kept screaming. It really didn't seem like the time to stop. Guy's mother began complaining bitterly when she was pulled away from my hands.

Then someone reached over the side of the balcony and said, "Take my hand. I'll pull you up."

And then, amazingly, Detective O'Shea did.

"What exactly did you think you were doing?" Detective O'Shea yelled at me.

"I was afraid they were going to leave town."

"Just for future reference, they have a police department in Fresno and they've been known to cooperate with the LAPD."

"Thanks. I didn't really know that." I guess I should have been able to figure it out, though.

"Which is exactly why you should have minded your own business!"

"I did call you. Several times."

"I don't care!" he was still yelling. But then he stopped, which was somehow even worse. "You seem blissfully unaware that there's more to this than simply figuring out what happened. We're going to have to go into a courtroom and prove beyond a reasonable doubt that the Petersons killed Guy. Now, do you know what you are?"

Oh crap. "Reasonable doubt?"

"Exactly."

"But, Cindy tried to kill me. Isn't that attempted murder?"

"It is. But her defense attorney will say that you accidentally fell over the balcony and she was trying to save you. They'll say that you're really the one who killed Guy Peterson and that everything you did was to throw suspicion onto Cindy."

"But none of that's true. And Cindy did kill her brother."

"I know that. But a jury won't. If they even *think* it's possible that you killed Guy they'll let his sister off. You see how that works? You see how your interfering with my investigation causes problems."

"Yes, sir," I said. I didn't need to sir him, but somehow it seemed appropriate. "Detective O'Shea? You're still holding my hand."

We were still on the balcony, too, and, yes, he was still holding the hand he'd pulled me up by. I didn't mind. It was kind of nice. Except for the fact that he was mad at me, and my hand was killing me. Actually, I was pretty sure both hands were a little bit broken.

He looked down at my hand, blushed and let it go. Then he led me inside the room, where a half a dozen uniforms were making sure the Petersons didn't go anywhere. The three of them sat on the edge of one bed looking sullen and silent.

They glared at me as O'Shea gave instructions to a uniform. When he turned his attention back to me, I asked, "Could someone go get me a bucket of ice?"

O'Shea gave me a questioning look.

"My hands are killing me."

"Someone go get a bucket of ice," he yelled.

One of the uniforms left the room. I frowned at O'Shea. "Um, do we have to stand right here?"

I mean, I was two feet away from someone who'd just tried to kill me. It wasn't exactly comfortable.

"No. We don't." O'Shea led me out into the hallway.

"Thanks," I said. "So…where have you been all day?"

"Interviewing Trailblazers. Gathering evidence."

I felt a little bad about that, but then I remembered something. "Oh, so you need to get someone over to Guy's apartment. There's a spot on the wall where they practically rubbed the paint off cleaning it. And then, there's blood in the cracks of the hardwood floors."

"And, did you contaminate my crime scene?"

"Not a lot." That was kind of a lie, since I did touch everything without gloves on. My fingerprints were probably everywhere. And they were probably the only ones.

The uniform arrived with a bucket of ice and I sat down on the floor and slipped my hands into it. They already looked swollen and I thought I might have dislocated a finger. It was a good thing I had a doctor's appointment on Friday.

O'Shea stepped away for a moment and spoke to a uniform, presumably about Guy's apartment. Then he stepped back over to me. "I'll need you to make a statement, but we can wait until tomorrow. In the meanwhile, between the time you entered the room and the time they threw you over the balcony—"

"Cindy. Cindy threw me over the balcony."

"Okay. Did the Petersons implicate themselves in any way?"

"Yes, repeatedly."

"Good. What did they say?"

"They talked about Cindy shooting her brother and how annoying it was to clean it up. Cindy's the murderer. Her parents just helped her cover it up."

"And people say there's no such thing as good parenting any more. What else did you learn?"

"There was money. Hidden. They took it."

Another uniform came over and told O'Shea, "The ambulance is downstairs."

"Ambulance? Who got hurt?" I asked.

"You did," O'Shea said.

"It's for me? What if I say no?"

"Go ahead and say no. You're still going to the hospital."

"You can't make me."

"All right. How about I arrest you?"

"Arrest me for what?"

"Interfering with an investigation."

"But I was trying to help."

"Yeah, most judges add extra time for that."

I didn't think that was true. "You're just mad because I figured everything out before you did."

"I would have figured it out and you know what—no one would have ended up hanging off a building."

"That really wasn't my fault. I was pushed."

"No, it was completely your fault for sticking your nose in where it didn't belong."

"Honestly, I was planning to stay in my room, but Cindy—"

"You came to the hotel. You had no business coming to the hotel. You can figure that out, can't you? The minute you walked into the building you were in the wrong."

I wasn't going to win this argument, so I agreed to go downstairs and get into the ambulance.

21

LOUIS AND MARC TRIED TO HAVE ANOTHER PARTY FOR ME, but I absolutely put my foot down. I'd called them to come pick me up from the emergency room at Cedars-Sinai that night and drive me back to Le Mondrian. It was nearly midnight and I was exhausted and a little disoriented. I had jammed several fingers and dislocated one. Remarkably, none were broken. They wrapped my hands in ace bandages and gave me a shot of Demerol.

"Are you sure you can drive like that?" Marc asked.

"Yeah, I'm fine."

"Why don't you drive Noah's car for him," Louis suggested.

"Yeah, I think I'd better."

"I'm fine," I said, then semi-passed out in the backseat of the Infiniti.

Thursday night we had a quiet dinner with Leon and I told them all everything that had happened.

"I can't believe you went to their hotel," Marc said. "That's so brave."

"No, it isn't. Not really. Actually, it has been pointed out to me that it was kind of stupid."

"Well, you had a much more interesting evening than I did," Leon said. "I watched *Doogie Howser* and fell asleep before the end. Now I'll never know whether he decided to cure cancer or teenage acne. He was struggling with the decision when I nodded off."

Louis had made pasta tossed in lemon and oil with roasted vegetables. It was delicious when I managed to get a bite. Handling a fork with my fingers taped together was a challenge. As was picking up a wine glass.

"Should one of us feed you?"

"Oh, please no. I'm actually not that hungry." And the thing is, I wasn't. The easiest food for me to eat with my hands messed up was cookies. So I'd eaten half a bag of Oreos that afternoon while watching Bette Davis in *Now, Voyager*. The story of an ugly-duckling spinster who falls in love with a married man was exactly what I needed after nearly being killed. "I could use a straw, though." That way I didn't have to pick up the wine glass.

Louis jumped up and ran into the apartment. It was nice to have friends with a fully stocked kitchen. He was back moments later dropping a cocktail straw into my wine glass.

"Thank you," I said.

"Well," Leon said. "I think it's something of a coincidence that the two murders were not connected."

"But they were connected," I said. "If Guy hadn't killed Gaines and set fire to the store his family would never have come here. If they hadn't come here they wouldn't have found the money, so there'd have been no reason for his sister to kill him."

"Do you really think she killed him for the money?" Leon asked.

"I think there was a big dose of sibling rivalry in there, too."

"And…" added Marc. "If Ted Bain had never witnessed the Pachuk murder none of it would have happened."

"I don't know about that," Louis said. "Guy would have found someone else to blackmail. He was doomed to end up a murder victim sooner or later."

"But that would have been a different story," I pointed out.

Louis brought out dessert, a blueberry pie he'd made from scratch with vanilla Häagen-Dazs.

"I thought you didn't make fancy things on school nights," I said.

"Well, this is a special occasion. Our favorite upstairs neighbor is alive and well." Then, as he was serving me a piece, Louis looked behind me and under his breath said, "Don't look now, but Detective Tall, Dark and Menacing is here."

I turned around and saw O'Shea standing in the courtyard. It was a disconcerting sight. I got up and went over to him.

"What are you doing here?"

"I wanted to see how you are."

I held up my bandaged and bruised hands and said, "I'm fine. I have a little trouble with cutlery and a lot of trouble with glasses. I've been providing my friends with a comedy show."

"Look. I want to say I'm sorry about yelling at you yesterday."

I shrugged. "You were right about most of it."

"I know. But I didn't have to be so pissy saying it."

"Well, thanks."

"And I wouldn't have arrested you if you didn't get in the ambulance."

"I figured."

"I mean, if you ever interfere again I might have to…"

"That's good to know."

"I should really stop talking about arresting you. Kind of strikes the wrong tone."

"The wrong tone for what?"

"Oh, um, well… I was wondering if you'd like to go see a movie sometime next week?"

"I own a video store. I usually wait for video."

"Oh, okay, well how about dinner?"

"You mean like a date?"

"Yes, like a date."

"I didn't know—I didn't realize you were gay."

"It's kind of a new thing. Well, not new. It's just… I haven't told too many people. My sister. That's about it."

Now I felt bad given what I had to say, "I'm sorry. I can't."

"Oh, okay."

"Can you tell me why?"

"No."

My doctor's office was Beverly Hills adjacent, on Robertson just below Burton Way. Becker-Morse Medical Group was on the second floor of a pink granite office building, which was only partially occupied. The clean white hallways had an other-worldly feel after driving through the grit of L.A. traffic. I walked through the varnished wood double doors and told the receptionist I was there.

The waiting room was done in mauve and a kind of turquoise that someone convinced them went with the mauve, but it really didn't. I took a seat and picked up *Rolling Stone*. Def Leopard was on the cover. Their story was all about the tragedies that had befallen the band. Drug overdoses, car accidents, the mumps. I knew their name but couldn't think of a single song of theirs. I skipped over an article about the music industry and AIDS, and went right to one about the governor of Arkansas running for president. I was struggling to figure out if the writer was pro or con when the nurse opened the door and called my name.

He was a stocky, possibly Italian-American guy in a loose-fitting pair of light blue scrubs. He had my file in one hand. It was a half-inch thick already. On the way to the exam room we stopped at a scale. I got on. He moved the weights back and forth until he got a number he liked. He wrote it down.

"You've lost some weight. Are you eating?"

"Yes," I said, though honesty I didn't think about it much.

"Well, try to keep your weight up."

Silly me, I thought, *here I'd been trying not to get killed.*

We went into exam room five. He took my blood pressure, my temperature, my pulse. He wrote each down but didn't comment. I hoped that meant I passed.

"Anything specific I should mention to the doctor?"

I held up my hands.

"Did you take a fall?"

"Sort of."

"And you went to the emergency room?"

"Yes."

"Okay, Dr. Morse will look over everything." The nurse got up. "He'll be in shortly." He smiled and left.

On the wall in front of me was a magazine rack. *Time* had a cover about the riots. Somehow they seemed to have happened a very long time ago. Had it only been two weeks? Two and a half? I suppose I'd seen a few boarded up businesses on the drive from Silver Lake but hadn't given them much thought. I imagined things were much worse in South Central, but for most of Los Angeles it was a wound that had opened and then almost immediately begun to close. I couldn't tell whether that was a good thing or a bad thing; a strength or a weakness.

Dr. Samuel Morse came into the exam room. He was blond and even-featured, good-looking enough to sail through life. I imagine some of his patients got "sick" just to come see him— just like people had taken Guy Peterson's photography class to see him. It didn't hurt that Dr. Morse asked everyone to call him Dr. Sam.

He said hello and asked, "What happened to your hands?"

"I had a sort of accident."

He took my hands in his and looked them over. "Did they give you any pain meds?"

"Tylenol with codeine."

"That's all I'm offering you."

I shrugged. "They don't hurt as much as they did."

"If the pain gets worse, call me. Otherwise you should be better every day."

He stepped over to the counter and opened my file, then read a few things and said, "Hmmmph."

"What?"

"Four-seventy."

"Oh, I see."

I'd known for a while that if my T-cells went below 500 I'd have to go on AZT. I didn't know how I felt about it. Certainly, my doctor was telling me it was a wise decision. But, was it? Jeffer had been on AZT and it hadn't helped. He'd waited so long to confirm that he had AIDS, though. And then there were things I'd been reading—

"Noah?"

Dr. Sam held out a couple of prescriptions.

"Oh, sorry." I took them, folded them and put them into my shirt pocket.

"One is for AZT three times a day and the other is for Bactrim which is just once a day."

"Thank you."

We were quiet for a moment. Then he said, "It doesn't mean anything specific. You're at the beginning of what will probably be a very long road."

"It doesn't feel that way."

"I know. But things are happening more quickly now. I'm sure there will be a cure in a couple of years. We'll get you there, don't worry."

Then we were done. I went back to the front and paid my co-pay. Walked out into the pristine hallway and pressed the elevator button. *How did I get here?* I wondered. Even though I knew, it still didn't really make sense.

When I met Jeffer we were okay. I mean, we thought we were okay. *I* thought we were okay. We were monogamous so we didn't bother with safe sex. Except Jeffer said he was okay, when he wasn't.

Sometime late in eighty-nine I remember we were getting dressed, after sex I think, though I don't really remember. I noticed a quarter-sized purple stain on the back of his right calf.

"What is that? I've never noticed it before."

"You haven't? It's a birthmark. It's always been there."

"It has?"

"Yes. You're usually paying attention to things a bit further up."

I should have known, though, should have recognized the stain for what it was. Especially when there was another and another. Less than a year later it was obvious he was sick. And it was obvious why.

I finally got him to admit, in a brief moment of honesty, that he'd known. That he'd had it all along; and that he'd known. Though to be fair, he'd barely admitted it to himself. I left him. Though, never completely. I couldn't let him die alone, but I couldn't forgive him.

On the way home, I stopped at a Rite-Aid and filled the prescriptions. The pharmacist seemed frightened when I handed her a ten-dollar bill for my co-pay. I imagine she went and washed her hands in scalding water as soon as I left.

I went home and put the pills in the medicine cabinet and left them there. I wasn't ready to take them. The next day I looked at them. And then the next. I was looking at them when the phone rang.

"Hello?"

"Did you ever get your taxes done?" my mother asked.

"I'm working on them."

"Don't wait until the last minute, Noah. An extension's not forever; they only give you six months."

"Yes, ma'am."

"You have to learn time management. Now that you're alone, you'll need to learn to do things on your own. Believe me, it was hard on me when your father died. I had no idea he did as much as he did. Honestly, I thought he just sat in his chair and drank beer. That sounds horrible, I know. I hope you don't think I'm speaking ill of your father, but it's true, he did just sit—"

I kept thinking about the pills. As soon as I took the first one that was it. I'd be taking them the rest of my life. However long that might be. It was an ending and a beginning all at once. And I'd gone through so many of those. I knew I had to try whether I really wanted to or not.

I went back to the medicine cabinet, cradled the phone between my neck and shoulder, and shook out a pill. One pill, three times a day. And one of the other. I poured a glass of water and took the first pill. And then the other.

"Noah!"

"What?" I asked, swallowing.

"I asked you a question."

"Sorry, what did you ask?"

"How was your week?"

"Oh, you know, same old same old."

Louis' Enchilada Casserole

Ingredient list:
- 18 corn tortillas
- 1 lb shredded chicken
- 1 small onion
- 1 cup chunky salsa
- 1 can enchilada sauce
- 1 can refried beans
- 1 lb shredded cheese
- 1 can mild jalapenos
- 1 tub sour cream
- ¼ cup milk or cream

Steps:

1. Find a really good Mercado that makes its own corn tortillas. Go early in the morning and make sure to buy them from the grandma, she'll give you the fresh ones. If you buy them from the daughter they'll be stale.
2. While you're at the Mercado, buy everything else you need.
3. When you get home, take out your biggest, deepest dish. I use one of those old orange Le Creuset baking dishes that I got at Out of the Closet. I tell people it was my mother's, giving it sentimental value. Spread olive oil all over the dish.
4. Preheat oven 375 degrees.
5. Preferably you have leftover chicken from the capon you roasted on Sunday. If you don't, throw a combination of chicken thighs and breasts into a crock pot add a can of stewed tomatoes and some spices and cook on low for about six hours.

6. Once the chicken is shredded you can begin to construct the casserole. Spread half the can of refried beans along the bottom of the pan. Top that with six tortillas. Spread out about a third of the chicken on top of the tortillas. Then some jalapenos, some diced onion and chunky salsa. Then a third of the cheese. Repeat until you have three layers.
7. Mix together the sour cream and milk until you have a loose mixture. Pour over the top of the casserole.
8. Cook for about 45 minutes or until bubbling.

Also By Marshall Thornton

The Perils of Praline

Desert Run

Full Release

The Ghost Slept Over

My Favorite Uncle

Femme

Praline Goes to Washington

Aunt Belle's Time Travel & Collectibles

IN THE BOYSTOWN MYSTERIES SERIES

The Boystown Prequels

Boystown: Three Nick Nowak Mysteries

Boystown 2: Three More Nick Nowak Mysteries

Boystown 3: Two Nick Nowak Novellas

Boystown 4: A Time for Secrets

Boystown 5: Murder Book

Boystown 6: From the Ashes

Boystown 7: Bloodlines

Boystown 8: The Lies That Bind

Boystown 9: Lucky Days

Boystown 10: Gifts Given